A Creature
Was Stirring

By Tobias Wells

A CREATURE WAS STIRRING

HARK, HARK, THE WATCHDOGS BARK

HAVE MERCY UPON US

BRENDA'S MURDER

A DIE IN THE COUNTRY

HOW TO KILL A MAN

THE FOO DOG

WHAT TO DO UNTIL THE UNDERTAKER COMES

DINKY DIED

THE YOUNG CAN DIE PROTESTING

DIE QUICKLY, DEAR MOTHER

MURDER MOST FOULED UP

DEAD BY THE LIGHT OF THE MOON

WHAT SHOULD YOU KNOW OF DYING?

A MATTER OF LOVE AND DEATH

A Creature
Was Stirring

TOBIAS WELLS

PUBLISHED FOR THE CRIME CLUB BY

DOUBLEDAY & COMPANY, INC.

GARDEN CITY, NEW YORK

1977

Library of Congress Cataloging in Publication Data

Forbes, Stanton, 1923–
A creature was stirring.
I. Title.

PZ4.F69255Cr   [PS3556.067]   813'.5'4
ISBN: 0-385-07331-3
Library of Congress Catalog Card Number 76–50800

First Edition

For Hope and Hank
with thanks

'Twas the night before Christmas
and all through one house
a creature was stirring . . .
it wasn't a mouse.

The creature was deadly;
the creature, disguised,
seemed harmless, seemed kindly
'til you looked in its eyes.

—*Mercy Bird*

A Creature
Was Stirring

Somebody could make up a special calendar for cops. June, July and August could be bracketed together in orange print under the heading of HOT AND HUMID (and I don't necessarily mean weather) and then October 31 through January 2, distinguished by a bright red danger color, could be subheaded TROUBLE TIMES. That's because the end of the year holidays seem to brew more crime, said crimes coming in all varieties from misdemeanors to suicides and murders. TROUBLE TIME, all capitals, begins with Halloween.

Any man who's served on the police force longer than I (longer than fifteen years, three months, seventeen days, that is) assures me that October 31 was a real bitch in the "old days," but tricks played on Allhallows Eve in this day and age are no treat to me. That's because as chief of police of this town of thirty thousand I've learned to expect a rash of complaints from the itchy citizenry come November 1.

This November 1, my second as Wellesley's police chief, was no better than last year, but no worse either. I glanced over the police blotter. Five cars decorated with spray paint in the Mayo Road area; six awnings slashed on shop fronts on Central Street and a score of windows decorated with shaving cream, damn the aerosol era; trees on the high school campus entwined with dozens of rolls of toilet paper, damn what's left of the affluent society; somebody's 1966 heap pushed (or driven) into Longfellow Pond; Mrs. Clinton Roberts reported an alleged case of cruelty to children. . . . I stopped at that one, reread Sergeant Dennehy's report. Mrs. Clinton Roberts of Schaller Street telephoned the desk at 9:22 P.M. Mrs. Roberts alleged that her daughter and son, aged six and five, returned screaming from trick-or-treating. Mrs. Roberts said the children told her "an awful ghost" had chased them from the premises at 6 Schaller Lane. They were in hysterics, their mother reported, but when she suggested one of the "big kids" was responsible, the older child told her no, the ghost had been inside the house at 6 Schaller Lane. Mrs. Roberts was considerably agitated. . . .

My telephone rang. I picked it up. "Chief Severson."

"Chief Severson, this is Mrs. Clinton Roberts of Twenty Schaller Street. I want you to know that I am very upset, very upset indeed over an incident that happened last night."

"Yes, Mrs. Roberts. I was just reading the report. It's a shame that the children were frightened, I think you were right when you guessed it was one of the older kids . . ."

"I've spoken to Harold again this morning. Harold is six and quite precocious. I told Harold that whoever chased him and his sister was just an ordinary person dressed up in a sheet, playing a joke"—her voice grated on the word joke—"but he feels positive that it was a ghost. His sister, Alicia, she is five—well, almost five—refuses to get out of bed this morning, she says the ghost is waiting outside. I just want to make sure that you don't treat this as an ordinary complaint and do nothing about it. Whoever terrified my children is wicked, Chief Severson. Wicked and mentally deranged!" When she'd begun the conversation, Mrs. Roberts had sounded calm and rational, but as she'd gone along, her voice had gotten higher and higher, more and more ragged, a woman on an edge.

"I promise you we'll look into it, Mrs. Roberts"—I tried to sound soothing—"but little children often get things mixed up and if it was one of the bigger boys or girls, it's going to be pretty hard to find him unless the children can identify . . ."

"Don't you listen?" shrilled Mrs. Roberts. "It's someone inside that house at Six Schaller Lane!"

"Are the children sure? They're kind of young to remember addresses, especially in the darkness and excitement."

"It couldn't be any other house! Don't you know your town at all? There are nine houses on Schaller Street but there's only one house on Schaller Lane. We've only lived here ten months, but we seem to know our way around better than you do!"

I suppressed a sigh. "I'll try to get out today," I offered. "May I talk to the children?"

She was shocked. "Of course not! A policeman? I don't

want them to undergo another traumatic experience. You go see the people at Six Schaller Lane and give *them* a traumatic experience. You leave my children alone!" And she cut the connection, leaving me with my mouth open, saving me from a sarcastic reply that would have been more fuel for a fire, and foolish to boot.

I reached for the Town of Wellesley Registrar's List of Residents. Where was Schaller Lane, anyway? Schaller Street was in Precinct G, way out Washington Street at the South Natick boundary. There was no Schaller Lane listed. Was this a "paper" street? Throughout Wellesley certain old streets had never been accepted as legal ways by the town, since they dated from times before the town was organized. Usually there were no houses on these paper streets, but apparently Schaller Lane was an exception. Apparently. Should I send somebody out to check on it or go myself? Better wait and see what the morning brought. I went back to reading the blotter. A rock through a picture window on Weston Road; an electric pole down on Route 9, victim of a drunken driver, two people, including the drunken driver, taken to the Newton-Wellesley Hospital; a Breaking and Entering at Papa Gino's, also on Route 9, easterly, toward the Newton line; an attempted B and E at the Falls branch of the South Shore Bank, alarm signal tripped but no entry.

The efficient Miss Miller, inherited from former long-time Police Chief Terence, came in with coffee on a tray. Miss Miller was not only efficient, but unfailingly polite. Even so, I had the feeling she looked upon me as a young upstart. Well, I might be on the young side for a police chief, but there were times when, at thirty-seven, I felt pretty old. Such as when Lief, my son, insisted I pitch a tennis ball to him for hours while he tried to hit it with a plastic bat. He is almost five and has just discovered baseball.

"Have you ever heard of Schaller Lane?"

Miss Miller picked up the empty tray, I was sipping at my coffee. "That's the Draggon estate."

"The Dragon estate?"

"Draggon. D-R-A-G-G-O-N. A very old family, there are only two sisters left. Florence and Veronica. I don't think Veronica lives here anymore. She got married and Florence stayed home with the old folks."

I waited for more, but Miss Miller was turning to go.

"Are there any funny stories about this Florence Draggon?"

"Funny stories?" That was one of my problems with Miss Miller: we practically didn't speak the same language, we were always asking each other what we meant by repeating the question.

"Rumors of eccentric behavior?"

"Not that I know of. I haven't seen her in years. She was ahead of me in school. There wasn't anything wrong with her then."

I watched her go out, thinking there wasn't anything much wrong with any of us thirty years ago. And then I thought, Hell, I was just a kid thirty years ago. I was hung up on age of late—too old for comfort, too young for my job? Drop it, Severson, what will you do when you hit forty?

I sipped at my coffee. Miss Miller makes a good brew out of instant coffee, which was worth a gold star on her report card. They didn't put gold stars on report cards anymore—at least Lief never got any. If somebody spooked Lief, Brenda would turn tiger. If I got a chance, maybe I'd drive out South Natick way toward Schaller Lane. For public relations if for no other reason.

My office door opened, Miss Miller stuck her head in. "Mr. Hix," she announced succinctly.

I suppressed a groan, told her to tell him to come in. "Ask him if he wants some coffee."

"Don't mind if I do." Selectman Hugo Hix was almost as wide as my door and maybe three quarters as tall. His face was a sun-tanned moon (I suspected he used a sun lamp year-round) topped by a head of gray fuzz. He was always smiling and looking benevolent. How he looked didn't mean a damn, I'd found that out already.

"Morning, Chief." Hix put out a pudgy hand, which I shook. "How's the world treating you?" Selectman Hix spoke in clichés, giving a stranger the idea that he was on the dense side. That impression was inaccurate too.

"Sit down, Hugo." He'd insisted on being called Hugo from our first meeting ("Jesus, Knute, nobody calls me Mr. Hix, I wouldn't know who you were talking to!"). "The world seems to be treating me all right. Our Halloween hijinks were, by and large, of the milder variety."

Hugo shook his round head, and I realized who he

reminded me of: an old Charlie Brown! A fat, old, devious Charlie Brown. I filed that away to tell Brenda.

"What can I do for you this morning, Hugo?"

"Oh, my, yes. I shouldn't be taking up your valuable time like this. Nothing important, really. I just had a few things jotted down someplace . . ." And he began to search the pockets of his suit jacket. He always wore dark suits, they all looked alike, loose and wrinkled. He produced the paper at last, a grocery-store tape which he had scribbled on the back of. He couldn't seem to read his own handwriting.

"Electric what?" He peered at it. "Oh, electric pole." He beamed. "Now I remember. There's a pole down on Route Nine . . ."

"Yes, I know. A motorist struck it early this morning. He's in the hospital now, but he'll be charged . . ."

"Rod Avery," Hugo interrupted.

"Yes, Rod Avery." I flipped open the police blotter. "Address, 104 Emerson Road; age, twenty-three; occupation, student . . ."

"He's Laurie Avery's son."

"Yes. Charged with driving under the influence, this is the second drunken driving charge, he'll lose his license for . . ."

"Laurie does a lot of fine things for this town. There's hardly a charity drive where she isn't right in there, working her head off. And she's a past president of the Wellesley Woman's Club and the League of Women Voters and now she's a big wheel for the Newton-Wellesley Hospital

Aides." He managed to sigh and smile at the same time. "A fine woman, Laurie Avery. Raised her son single-handed after her husband was killed. Not an easy job for a woman alone."

I closed the blotter carefully. "What are you telling me? Rod Avery was loaded, he had a passenger in the car, a girl from Needham who probably will need some plastic surgery after her encounter with the windshield, he wrapped his car around an electric pole so that a whole section of town had a power outage, he's done it before and he didn't learn—what are you telling me?"

Hugo put up a conciliatory hand. "Now, now, don't get your back up, Knute. I know he's a spoiled smart-ass kid and you know it too, but it's his mother I'm thinking about. He's given her enough grief to last a lifetime already. I remember about eight years ago when he was in junior high they got him for vandalism at Woodlawn Cemetery—Jesus, breaking up tombstones, can you imagine? Well, I happened to be on the special force then so I was kind of in on things, and—well, Laurie Avery nearly went to pieces, she was so shook up. Andy Terence, course he knew her better than you do, do you know her?"

"Not personally."

Hugo nodded. "That's it, you see, that's it."

I gritted my teeth. "There isn't a thing I can do for him, Hugo. It's already gone into the registry. And he'll have to pay for the pole. How he'll make it up to the girl, I don't know."

"The registry, huh?" I could almost see the wheels turning in that round head. "Well, now, I do have some friends there. I did a lot of campaigning for the governor, you know, got to meet a lot of people. . . . As for the electric pole, he'll pay for that, of course. I'm all in favor of making the penalty fit the crime, and I wouldn't be at all surprised if Laurie wouldn't foot the bill for the girl's plastic surgery—if the insurance won't cover it." He put his hands out in an expansive gesture. "All things being taken care of, you'd go along, wouldn't you?"

"What about Rod Avery?"

"What about him? He's got another year at Babson, he'll straighten out in time."

"Do you think so? Do you really think so? Eight years ago I guess Rod Avery got a slap on the wrist and that was that. The other drunken driving charge—that happened in Jamaica Plain so nobody could fix that soon enough, but it was a first offense and he only lost his license for a relatively short time, right? So what happens next time, Hugo? Some people can't learn easy lessons. You have to pound it into their heads."

Smiling, Hugo agreed. "You've told it like it is, Knute, that's for sure. But I do believe this time—I've just come from talking to Rod, I think this one scared the stuffing out of him. If you'll go along, I don't think we'll have any trouble from him. If we do"—he raised fat hands in a gesture of that's that—"I'll be right behind you in throwing the book at him."

The coffee I'd drunk didn't sit well. God, I hated this

kind of crap. "I won't raise a hand," I told Hugo, "one way or another. That's the best I can do for you."

Hugo beamed. "Can't ask for more than that." He peered at his list again. "Now, let's see . . . I tell you, my handwriting's getting worse and worse, L-E-E-C-H? Now what . . . oh, I know. B-E-E-C-H. Stanley Beech, you know Stanley? No? Well, Stanley comes from one of Wellesley's old families, but he's kind of fallen on bad times. Stanley lives down on Stonecleve near Morse's Pond. Now, Stanley's got a dog he thinks the world of, a Great Dane getting along in years who wouldn't hurt a fly. Seems that a new family on Russell Road called the dog officer complaining that Stanley's old dog had nipped one of their kids. Wrote a letter to the selectman, too, the Aborns did—that's the name of the new family. Now, I know that Kirkham checked it out like he always does, Kirkham's certainly a conscientious dog officer, but I think he missed a point or two here when he recommended that Stanley's dog be restrained. I looked into the matter personally and it seems that the Aborn kid, named Homer—the names some people give their kids—it seems that Homer Aborn was trespassing on Stanley's property . . ."

I let him drone on. Lately I'd been thinking that it might be a real good idea to keep some kind of record of Hugo's requests, just in case the sky fell in one day. I wondered, as I had so many times before, how Kendall Owens and Alfreda Burke, the other two selectmen, let Hugo get away with his insidious interference. Maybe I'd find out one day, but in the meantime . . .

He was folding up the grocery tape, saying, "I guess that takes care of it this morning. Things are running so smoothly I only had a couple of little chores this week. You're doing a good job, Knute, a real good job. I want you to know that."

I nodded my thanks. We shook hands and he reached for the door. If I was lucky, no one would come in until he got out.

"Bye, Hugo, have a pleasant day."

"I'll try, Knute, I'll try. But I've got an awful lot to do, I'm a very busy man, you know. When I ran for selectman I told the voters that, since I live and work in the town, I could give them my full attention, twenty-four hours a day, seven days a week, and I tell you I honor that commitment . . ."

We were off again but fortune smiled and my phone rang. I waggled my fingers at Hugo in farewell and picked up my telephone, letting my relief show in my voice when I answered.

"Knute," said my wife, Brenda, "would you mind having lunch downtown today? Anne called, there's a sale at Lord & Taylor's in Chestnut Hill and if I go now I can be back by the time Lief has to be picked up at nursery school."

South Natick is a small village, a physically separated part of Natick proper, that dates back to prerevolutionary days. Its Eliot Street turns into Wellesley's Washington Street at the town line and just after the town line lay Schaller Street on my right.

I drove slowly along Schaller, less than a dozen houses backed along the river, then the road took an abrupt right turn and just at the elbow I saw a homemade signpost that read Schaller Lane.

The house sat directly at the end of the short macadam street. Beyond the house was the river and along the sides stood a small forest of firs, pines and blue spruce. I wheeled into a gravel driveway alongside the building. The house was clapboard, painted gray. The windows, and there were many of them, rather narrow ones, two panes over one, sparkled in the November sun.

Across the front of the house ran a veranda with a Victorian-style railing that disappeared around the left side. On the right was an odd, semicircular room. The roof was peaked three times, two on either side of the narrow front, the central one higher above the door, and even the roof shingles were gray—not a faded, weathered gray, but a well-painted, well-maintained chosen-on-purpose gray. Everything was tidy, steps swept, porch clean, lawn beyond raked of the leaves that had fallen. Big trees mixed in with the tall firs, maples and elms; they'd been there a long time.

The doorbell was an old-fashioned one—there was a handle that one turned, and the sound jangled shrilly inside.

Very quiet here, I thought. I could hear the murmur of the river.

The door opened suddenly and I looked into the face of a woman whose short white hair stood up in spikes, whose small blue eyes glittered and whose hand brandished a large wooden spoon. "Do you like gingerbread?" she demanded in a breathless voice.

"Gingerbread? Sure . . ."

"Come in then." She reached for me, caught my jacket sleeve and tugged. I crossed the threshold thus, almost involuntarily, then followed her as she trotted through three rooms filled with heavy furniture and God knows what else—I had only the impression of crowding, until we emerged into the fourth room, a long kitchen dominated by a giant black stove. The woman—Miss Draggon? —snatched up a hot pad and opened the oven door. Heavenly smells came out, and I realized how long it had been since I'd smelled fresh gingerbread.

"Ah," said my hostess with satisfaction. She exchanged the wooden spoon for a second hot pad, withdrew a big oblong pan and carried it to a marble-topped counter. "Sit down," she commanded without looking at me. I sat.

A plate holding gingerbread appeared before me and I promptly bit into a spicy square. It tasted just as good as it smelled.

"Now," said the woman, "what can I do for you? I hope you're not selling magazines."

Swallowing, I shook my head. When I could, I said, "Chief Severson, ma'am, from the Wellesley police."

"Oh, really?" Her small bright eyes widened and she sat across from me. "What on earth do you want?"

"You're Miss Draggon?"

"Certainly. Florence Draggon. Have another piece of gingerbread. Veronica doesn't care for it."

"Veronica?"

"My sister. Mrs. Digby. She lives with me. Since her husband died." She leaned forward. "Has Veronica misbehaved?"

"Were you home last night? When the trick-or-treaters came around?"

Miss Draggon blinked. "What a peculiar question. Are you sure you are who you say you are? I haven't seen any identification."

Miss Draggon was a little hard to follow. I took out my wallet and showed her the gold badge they'd given me when I became chief. She looked it over, handed it back and said, "Let's go sit in the parlor, Chief—Severson, did you say? It's much more formal there. What happened to Chief Terence? I thought he'd be chief forever. Like Franklin Delano Roosevelt."

I started to say the kitchen was good enough for me, but she was on her way so I followed her through the dining room (a big long table had ten chairs arranged around it and there was room for more) into a room I took to be a living room (the walls were decorated with many pictures of stern-looking old people—ancestors, I judged) but Miss Draggon kept on going until we reached the room at the front of the house where I understood what she meant by "parlor." The sofas—there were two, one on each long wall—had brocaded upholstery and high backs framed in fancy carved wood. The outer wall was rounded—it was that odd-shaped room I'd seen from out-side.

In one corner stood a huge handsome piece of furniture like a very thick table on very heavy legs. The color of the wood was a pinky-gold and it was beautifully grained. Miss Draggon saw me looking at it and explained, "It's rosewood. My grandmother's piano."

"Many of our pieces are old," she said, looking around in satisfaction. "The Draggons never threw anything out."

"Yes. Well . . ." We were getting off the track, I came back to it. "As I was saying, when the trick-or-treaters came last night . . ."

"Oh, but nobody came."

I stared at her. She stared back with her little blue eyes, so bright they looked as though tiny lights might be shining behind them.

"Don't you believe me?" she asked. "Come. I'll show you." And she was off again, this time heading toward the front hall. There on a table stood two big wooden bowls. One held gingerbread men, homemade, obviously; the other, shiny red and yellow apples. "We were all ready, but nobody came. Nobody ever comes. I think they're afraid of us. Maybe they think the house is haunted."

"Two little kids—very little kids, five and six years old —didn't ring your doorbell?"

"Not while I was downstairs."

"You weren't downstairs all evening?"

"No. I went up about eight-thirty. Veronica was watch-ing a program on television that I particularly dislike."

I hadn't asked Mrs. Roberts what time the children had gone out, but eight-thirty seemed pretty late for little ones. "Where is your sister? Could I speak to her?"

"She's gone to Natick. To the doctor's, I think, although I'm not sure. She says she has shingles. I tell her she's always been a hypochondriac."

"When do you expect her back?"

She waved her plump little hands. "I haven't any idea. Before the last bus, I suppose."

"Bus?"

"Yes. We haven't a car. Or, rather, we do have a car. In the garage. It was Papa's, a 1922 Essex, but it isn't registered. And I have a hunch the tires are rotted through after all these years. Besides, I don't drive."

I found an impulse to laugh. There was something about Miss Florence Draggon that amused me; maybe she was the last of the cheerful nuts. But not if she frightened children—hell, I wasn't even sure it hadn't been a case of vivid imagination with the Roberts kids.

"Did some children say they came here?" asked Miss Draggon.

I nodded.

"And something bad happened?"

"What makes you ask that?"

"Well, you are the chief of police. I don't suppose you go around asking questions when something good happens. I wonder if Veronica did put on her costume."

"What costume?"

"Oh, we have an attic full of costumes. When we were

young, we had all sorts of gay times. Parties. When we were young. She was saying last night how much fun Halloween used to be, how she'd like to dress up and go trick-or-treating. I told her she was much too old for that. She's three years older than I, you see, even if she does dye her hair black."

"What kind of costume might she have put on?"

Miss Draggon shrugged. "I don't know, really. If she did. She might have. We have all kinds." She looked thoughtful. "Maybe a ghost? No—I don't think—maybe the headless woman?"

"The headless woman?"

"Yes. Very clever. We took an old black taffeta dress belonging to Grandmother, Grandmother was a tall woman, and we cut holes for eyes and you just put the neck of the dress over your head . . ." She laughed. "I remember when Veronica wore that. She had a crush on Evan Cawley that year and when he came to the door . . ." She laughed again. "He ran all the way down Schaller Street. I watched him from the upstairs window!"

"Yes, she might have done that. I'd really like to talk to Mrs. Digby, Miss Draggon. When do you think I might find her home?"

"Why, anytime. This evening. Tomorrow. Tell me when you're coming and she'll be expecting you." She smiled. "She likes to talk to handsome young men. I'm afraid she's always been a bit of a flirt."

The idea of a Miss Draggon type acting flirtatious reminded me that I was making a good deal out of very little. "We've had a complaint that some children were frightened last night by someone in this house. I presume it was your sister dressed up in the headless costume. Kindly tell her for me that a telephone apology to the children's mother might be in order. Her name is Mrs. Roberts, on Schaller Street."

Miss Draggon lost her smile. "Oh, dear, I am sorry. Veronica can be—rather childish herself. I'll speak to her, I promise. Do you have any children, Chief Severson?"

"One son."

"If I find a paper bag, would you take him some ginger-bread men?" She glanced at the full bowl. "It's a shame to let them go to waste."

I felt a sudden pity for her. Odd old girl, baking gingerbread for children who never came. A spinster, probably longing for children she'd never had. "Sure. Thanks. He'd love them."

Her smile returned, her blue eyes regained their sparkle. "I'll be right back." She took the bowl with her and returned with a large brown bag of gingerbread, much too much for one small boy, but I took it and thanked her and went out to my car. I sat for a minute, listening to the ripple of the water from behind the house and the raucous cry of a blue jay. It was a quiet place; I might have been in the country rather than in the fashionable suburb of Wellesley.

As I backed out, I looked up at the house and saw Miss Draggon standing at one of the sidelights of the door. She waved. I waved back and drove off. I spotted the Roberts house, number twenty; it was neatly fenced, and two children in corduroy pants and jackets were playing in the yard. I'd let Miss Draggon and her sister smooth things over. Mrs. Roberts could have saved me a lot of trouble if she'd gone to 6 Schaller Lane herself.

❖❖❖❖❖❖❖❖

I had my lunch at Chin's Village. I was in the mood for Chinese food and Paul Chin and his staff turn out a good meal, which is no doubt why I ran into town counsel Gary Lyons with three other guys, two of whom I knew slightly.

"Hey, Knute!" Gary motioned to me to come over. "You know Kendall Owens and Bill Sowerby, don't you? And Chip Dawher?"

"I know Mr. Owens and Mr. Sowerby." I nodded to them. "But I haven't had the pleasure of meeting Mr. Dawher." I put out my hand. "I know who you are, of course." He was the editor of the newspaper.

"And I know who you are, of course," replied Dawher. "Join us, why don't you?"

Kendall Owens, selectman and thus another of my bosses, was a Boston-based lawyer who lived in Wellesley, low-key and seemingly sound of reason, a good-looking guy. Brenda thinks he looks like a young Cary Grant. A young Cary Grant and an old Charlie Brown—and who did Alfreda Burke remind me of? Alfreda Burke—no other!

"Let's get together after Wellesley Club," Owens said. He glanced at me. "Are you coming, Knute?"

I knew about Wellesley Club, of course. I wasn't a member, but I'd been told there was a long waiting list. I shook my head.

"Oh, you should," he said. "Gary, bring him along, why don't you? Would Mrs. Severson like to come? It's lady's night. Alfreda's the speaker."

"I'll ask her," I said.

"I'll have Edith call her," Lyons offered.

"Thanks. I've got to run along." I counted out what I thought I owed plus extra for a tip.

"You know what they say"—Dawher sounded just a little furry of tongue, he'd had three martinis if I figured right—"a policeman's work is never done."

"You mean a woman's work is never done." Kendall and I stood, he put out his hand for me to shake. "Chip's wife can't be a women's libber or he'd never make that mistake."

"No," I agreed, "the way it goes is—a policeman's lot is not a happy one."

❖❖❖❖❖❖❖❖

"Doddy, is that you?" Mrs. Miller's voice was on the breathy side, she suffered from emphysema as well as arthritis.

"Yes, Mother." Doddy thought again, did not say again, who else could it be?

"How was your day?"

"Fine, Mother. How was yours?" She half-listened to the reply, finished unbuttoning her coat, hung it up in the hall closet. She removed the kitted gray hat from her head, placed it on the closet shelf. Shutting the closet door, she picked up the shopping bag she'd placed on the oriental runner and, smiling, walked the two paces down the narrow hall and turned left into the living room. She bent to kiss her mother's wrinkled but soft cheek and said, "Hello, Polly," to the small green parrot in the cage nearby.

"Yawk, cracker, Polly wants . . ." Perhaps it was her fault that Polly's vocabulary was so limited, but how did one go about training a parrot to speak?

Mother Miller was dressed in her favorite dressing gown, green velvet and lace, at least twenty years old but carefully preserved, like Mother. She had rouge on her furrowed cheeks and lipstick on a mouth, the lines of which had blurred over the years. Doddy's mother had always paid great attention to her appearance, it had annoyed Doddy when she was younger (vanity, vanity!) but she'd learned to live with it.

"Well, how was he today?" her mother asked.

Doddy didn't need to ask who "he" was. She shrugged. "Same as usual. Polite. Icily polite, I should say." She sniffed. "I was wondering if he bleaches his hair."

"You think so?" Mother was fascinated. If you wanted to amuse Mother you told her gossip or described the latest fashions at the Triangle Shop.

Doddy shrugged again. "I'd better put the groceries in the refrig, Mother. I've got a surprise for dinner."

Mrs. Miller giggled girlishly, waving her curled hands gaily. "T-bone steaks, Doddy? Tell me it's T-bone steaks."

"No, not T-bone steaks. They're much too dear. It's shrimp. I'm going to make a nice shrimp casserole, you'll like that."

Now it was Mrs. Miller's turn to sniff. "That's expensive too. I don't see why we can't ever have T-bone steaks. When you father was alive . . ."

Because, thought Doddy on her way to the kitchen, it's not easy to slip a T-bone steak into your pocketbook, that's why. Small cans of shrimp off the gourmet rack were another matter—quite simple. Although one must be careful, very careful. For Doddy Miller to be caught in the act of shoplifting (yes, might as well put the name to the deed) would be catastrophic. But therein lay the pleasure, the thrill. She shivered with remembered excitement and set to work in the kitchen. When the casserole was in the oven, she poured two glasses of rosé (a good brand, taken from the wine alcove at Lilja's package store) and took·one in to her mother. Mrs. Miller's glass was not a stemmed glass, because she had trouble holding one of those. Doddy used a tumbler for her, a tumbler with a cloth coaster that fitted around like a sock. Mother often fussed about the arrangement ("Can't see the color of the wine, Doddy, that's half the fun.") but tonight she sipped and said nothing.

"Did Dr. Ziggler come today?"

"Yes." Docile, suspiciously docile.

"Did he give you some new pills?"

Glancing toward the window, she said, "It looks windy out. Do you think it will snow? So early? Smells like snow to me."

"Mother. Did Dr. Ziggler give you some new pills?"

"Yes."

"And did you take them today?"

"Yes."

"Mother!"

"Well, I did. Of course I did. But all his pills and shots aren't doing me a bit of good, I don't see why you don't take me into Boston and find an acupuncture specialist . . ."

The telephone rang stridently. It was conveniently placed by Mrs. Miller's chair, so she had to interrupt her acupuncture speech (she should make a tape or, better still, a long-playing record) to answer it. She used her telephone voice, sweet, coy. "Hello. Who's calling please?"

Why did she always answer the telephone like that? It was so embarrassing. At one time Doddy had remonstated with her, but she'd explained that all sorts of terrible people made telephone calls these days and it was better, much, to know immediately who was calling, so Doddy gave up.

"Oh, Hugo! How nice to hear your voice. You'll want to speak to Doddy, I imagine. No one cares to talk to an old relic such as I." This was followed by the girlish giggle.

Doddy reached for the phone, but Mother was listening, smiling, "Flatterer! Flattery will get you everywhere with me, you know. You are a rogue, Hugo. Why don't you stop by and see us sometime? The telephone was a terrible invention, if you want my opinion. I'd much rather see friends face to face than talk to them on a machine."

Doddy suppressed a sigh. She felt resentment, followed by guilt. Who did Mother have to talk to? . . . Dr. Ziggler, Clarice, who came from Dorchester one day a week to clean, and Doddy herself. Patience, Doddy. What a hateful word along with duty.

Mother was handing her the phone. Never any privacy either. "Hello, Hugo. What can I do for you?" He wanted something, of course; he always wanted something.

"That's what I like about you, Doddy, my girl, always straight to the point, all business. I tell you, if everybody came to the point like you do, we'd have a much more efficient world, but unfortunately . . ."

"It's just that I have dinner on the stove," she interrupted.

"Yes, of course. It is that time, isn't it? I swear I get so busy helping my friends and the town that time just gets away from me. Tell you what I thought, Doddy, it's about the blotter. I haven't been able to look it over lately the way I used to, when good old Chief Terence was at the helm, you know. This new fellow, Severson, seems to think that a monthly report from the department is sufficient, but I tell you that an ounce of prevention is worth a pound of cure, you know what I mean? Say I see a little item that indicates some lad is going in the wrong direction. Say I know his father or his mother and I go to them and set the boy back on the right track. I've done it many a time, I can tell you, but I don't need to tell you, you know that. Only how can I continue if I can't see the blotter and get after it before it's too late, before he's been brought to court in Needham, a mark against the lad all his life? How can I help if I don't know what's going on?"

Chief Severson had closed the blotter, the official blotter with names and addresses, to anyone other than those in the department, and one of Doddy's new tasks was the copying of calls, investigations and arrests into a second book that eliminated pertinent details that Severson

thought were no one else's business, including the selectmen.

"Chief Severson keeps the blotter in his safe, Hugo. I
should think you should speak to him . . ."

"Ummm, but, you see, that's it. I have. And he so much
as said that he was protecting the populace. Well, that's
right, certainly, don't bandy names about, no, indeed, but
I am, after all, one of the town fathers and as such . . .
well, you know that I mean. Now I was wondering if you
wouldn't like to join my little do-good society of one and
slip me a copy of the blotter from time to time, you've got
that new copying machine and it wouldn't take a minute."

"No, it wouldn't, Hugo, but I'd be disobeying my boss."
She felt her cheeks flush, that he would dare to presume
that she would spy like that. And besides, she'd heard
rumors—that there were times when money, or if not
money, favors, came Hugo's way after he'd visited a
mother or father on behalf of a lad going the wrong way.

There was a pause and Hugo cleared his throat. "Yes,
of course, I hadn't thought of it exactly that way. The
thing is, it might be breaking a rule, or bending a rule,
that's more like it, but for a good cause, you know. There
might even be"—another throat clearing—"a little something in it for you, Doddy. To recompense you for your
time and"—he laughed—"salve your conscience?"

"No, Hugo. I couldn't. You'll have to speak to Chief

Severson." Mother was making curious faces, and Doddy turned her back on her.

There was another laugh, along with a slight change of tone. Let him get his back up, what did Doddy care? She was on Civil Service and there was nothing Hugo Hix could do to her. "Well, I'm sorry you couldn't see things my way, Doddy. Maybe you'll change your mind when you think it over. You've got to break eggs to make an omelet, you know. Don't forget to invite your mother to the Thanksgiving Day do. And no hard feelings, eh, Doddy?"

"No hard feelings, Hugo."

"What did you mean, no hard feelings?" Mother was asking as she hung up the phone.

"Hugo wanted me to do something I can't do." She drained her wine glass, headed for the kitchen.

"What? What did he want you to do?" Mother's breathy voice followed her.

"I'd rather not discuss it, Mother." She rattled pans and set plates down hard to cover the muttering sounds from the living room. Polly decided to join in by demanding a cracker.

"Stubborn," said Mother, her bright red mouth set, when Doddy brought her tray to her. "You were always stubborn. Just like your father. I don't know what it was that Hugo asked you to do but he is, after all, a selectman and it might have done us some good, you know. If you'd just co-operate once in a while maybe we could have

T-bone steaks instead of this mush." And she shoved at the plate with her clawed hands, sent it tumbling off the tray onto the floor.

"Yawk, yawk," said Polly. "A cracker?"

❖❖❖❖❖❖❖❖

Brenda, pleased with herself, displayed a suede skirt she'd gotten at the Lord & Taylor sale. "At less than half price, Knute! Don't you think it's stunning?"

"Very nice." The gray color made me think of the Draggon house, which reminded me that I'd left the bag of gingerbread men in the car. I started out to get it but the telephone rang and it was for me.

"Chief Severson? This is Laurie Avery."

Oh, ho. "Yes, Mrs. Avery?"

"I just wanted to—I hope I'm not interrupting your dinner?"

"No."

"Good. I just wanted to say thank you."

"Thank you for what?"

"Hugo—Mr. Hix—told me how understanding you were

when he spoke to you about my son." Doubt shaded the clear bell-toned voice.

"If Mr. Hix told you I was understanding then he incorrectly reported our meeting. I was not—and am not—understanding. In my opinion, Mrs. Avery, your son is badly in need of discipline. If not self-discipline, then some other sort of discipline."

There was a pause, then coldly, "I see. I apologize for calling you, Chief Severson."

I was instantly ashamed of myself. I'd taken out my resentment of Hugo on a woman I'd never met. "I'm sorry, Mrs. Avery," I said quickly. "I didn't mean to be brusque. It's just that I resent being misquoted."

There was another pause. "Hugo—is capable of bending facts to suit him. Perhaps we should understand one another. He said you were willing to give Rod another chance. He said if I paid for the light pole and took care of the medical problems of the Means girl . . ." She let her voice trail off.

"That wasn't what I said at all, Mrs. Avery. Hugo suggested that money and influence would repair all damages. I replied, maybe not in so many words, that neither money nor influence had repaired the fault in Rod Avery. That's the way the conversation went."

This time she didn't reply, but she was still there, presumably listening, so I went on. "Mr. Hix spoke eloquently of the services you perform for this town. I told him that I wouldn't go out of my way to see that your son is properly punished; that was the affect of the entire conversation. So I guess you don't owe me any thanks."

"That's plainly put, Chief Severson." She cleared her throat. "Nonetheless, I do thank you for your time."

"In that case, you're welcome." I started to hang up.

"Chief Severson?"

"Yes?"

"If I could take some more of that time—could I make an appointment to talk to you about Rod? Whenever it's convenient?"

"I . . ." I started to say she'd better talk to someone better qualified, but I was pretty sure I heard a pleading note in that decisive voice. "Yes, of course, only I'm no psychologist, I'm just a cop, I don't know that I can help . . ."

"I'm willing to waste my time if you are."

"Sure. At ten tomorrow? At the station?"

Hesitation. "You couldn't come to my house?"

Too public for her at the station, I gathered. "All right. At ten."

"Now I can really say thank you."

"What was that all about?" asked Brenda when I'd hung up.

I made a face. "A counseling session." I told her about it. "I'm way out of place in this father-confessor bit."

"Laurie Avery." Brenda looked thoughtful.

"What about Laurie Avery?"

"She's so—assured. You wouldn't think she'd have a problem, at least not for long. She's—I don't know—so glossy. What was it the Indians said? Don't judge a man until you've walked a mile in his moccasins?"

I opened the refrigerator door and took out a can of beer. "Everybody's got problems, sugar. If I didn't know it before I took this job, I'm finding out now."

"Daddy!" Lief appeared in the kitchen doorway, his hands behind him. "Want to see what I drew?"

"I sure do. What did you drew?"

"I drew you!" And he held it out for me, a stick figure with a very large head, big, round, blue lopsided circles for eyes and yellow streaks for hair. Just below the chin, where a neck might be, was a four-pointed star and printed on it were the words "BIG CHEEFE."

Brenda, laughing, told me, "It looks just like you. Is that last word 'C-H-E-E-F-E' or 'C-H-E-E-S-E'?"

❖-❖-❖-❖-❖-❖

The Avery house was long and low, dormered; brick walls were painted white, but random unpainted bricks broke the monotony. I pushed the doorbell button, which caused a soft chiming inside.

She was on the short side but she made a tall impression. She wore tight-fitting jeans, faded blue but not denim, some kind of velvety fabric, with a simple blue silk shirt.

The hair was pale, pale blond, drawn back behind the neck, left hanging. She said, "Chief Severson?"

"Mrs. Avery?"

"Come in. I do appreciate your coming."

I followed her inside, walking on eggshell-tinted carpet. She was barefoot. I guessed her feet wouldn't be cold on rugs that thick.

The living room was what I expected. Almost white walls, drapes, more eggshell carpet. Low, sand-colored sofas, a pink-brick fireplace and one big abstract painting on one long wall.

"I thought you'd like some coffee." She arranged a tray, cups, saucers, spoons, a glass carafe atop a warming candle, and dull gold cream and sugar set.

"Thank you. Cream only, please."

The chair I sat in, ivory-brocaded, was the kind that welcomed a body so completely it would take an effort to get out. The coffee was absolutely noninstant. Mrs. Avery lit a cigarette. She sipped coffee and studied me with eyes more gold than hazel.

"I won't pretend that Rod is a solid citizen," she began at last. "But if you knew him . . ." She discarded that sentence, tried another. "A mother knows what she's brought, knows whether what's inside is good or bad."

I nodded politely. I'd heard this speech before,

different words maybe, but the same song: my son is a good boy!

She set the coffee cup down. "He adored his father. He was at exactly the wrong age when he was killed. If he'd been younger, he wouldn't have understood; older, he could have withstood the shock more easily, but he was fourteen." She smiled bleakly, stubbed out her cigarette in a shiny white ashtray. "A difficult age at best."

"What's he trying to do?" I asked. "Emulate his father? He drives like a racer, I'm told. Drunk or sober."

She lit another cigarette. "I—we—sought psychiatric help after the cemetery incident. The psychiatrist said he vandalized the gravestones because he was protesting the death of his father. Rod went to Dr. Porter two years, then he refused to go any longer. He told me that he understood himself, he didn't need a head-shrinker." Another wry smile. "His choice of words, naturally."

"And you accepted that?"

"Yes. He seemed so much better, happier."

"My reports indicate he was stopped for speeding, let off with a warning, a couple of years ago."

She nodded. "I know. I pretended"—she was choosing her words very carefully—"that it was normal for a young man. Andy—Chief Terence—was kind enough to call me, to alert me to the problem. Rod and I talked it over. We have no difficulty communicating." She stubbed out the second cigarette. "Maybe I'm mistaken."

"Do you think he's showing suicidal tendencies?"

She preferred to avoid that question, so she looked down, hiding her irritation. "Of course not!" With her anger controlled, she raised her eyes, looking again into mine. "I'm afraid it's my fault. I believe he is seeking attention. I've gotten rather involved with various causes, organizations. I'm afraid I've neglected him. But I intend to put that right." She reached out toward me. "I promise."

I put my empty cup down. She was quick to react. "More?"

"No, thank you. Your conclusions are thoughtful ones, but I'm curious. . . . You've been wrapped up in your causes for more than the past two years, Mrs. Avery. Why should your activities suddenly set your son off like an unmanned missile?"

The way she blushed was right in character. "Two years ago Rod assumed, incorrectly, that I was considering remarriage."

"I see." I did see; I'd been expecting something like that. "Apparently, the suspicion hasn't been laid to rest."

She didn't try to hide the anger this time. "I'm not a marble statue! Nor am I much past forty. I do see men upon occasion, but that doesn't mean I intend to marry any of them. I've told Rod time and time again." She lit another cigarette.

"But that's not enough to satisfy him." I made it a statement rather than a question.

"It seems not."

I looked at my watch; back at my office the department

budget waited like a crocodile in the sewer pipe. The sooner I attended to it, the better. "I understand your problem, Mrs. Avery, but I don't know what I can do about it."

The gold-beige eyes shone—unshed tears? "I just wanted you to understand that I am not one of those totally selfish mothers, that I am trying, Rod and I are trying." She jumped up, with her control resumed. "I simply thought you'd have more patience with my son if you understand that everyone is trying."

I stood too. "Mrs. Avery, I have as much compassion as the next guy. I'm also as susceptible to coffee and conversation with charming ladies. But if your son doesn't stop playing death on wheels, I'm going to see that he's without those wheels for a long, long time. Unless"—I reached for my coat, thrown over a side chair—"he goes by the book or unless"—I slid my arms into the sleeves—"he ends up spread all over the pavement, he's going to do a lot of walking, Mrs. Avery. You can tell him that for me."

She opened the door for me. "Have I done anything to offend you?"

"Not at all, Mrs. Avery. Thank you for the coffee."

Nerve, she had; did she have nerve. A little private chat, a little feminine charm and the new police chief would be a pussy cat just like the last one.

"Didn't you think she was lovely-looking?" asked Brenda during dinner.

"Uhmm. What did you do to the macaroni and cheese?"

"Used some cornmeal for texture."

"It's kind of dry."

"I know. It needs more milk. When I reheat it tomorrow it will be better. What was she wearing? She has such gorgeous clothes."

"I didn't notice. Pants. Like blue jeans. Did I remember to tell you about Monday? We're invited to the Wellesley Club. Edith Lyons will be calling you."

"Oh, really? But what am I going to wear?"

I didn't bother to answer that one, we'd been married six years and I'd learned there are some you just don't go after.

The phone rang. "I'll get it." Brenda put down her fork. She had a habit of keeping the public off me during meals, a habit I appreciated, but since I was through I waved her off.

"Hello?"

"Is this Chief Severson?"

"It is." Terence had had an unlisted phone, but I figured the public had a right to get in touch with the head of their police force.

"This is Mrs. Clinton Roberts of Schaller Street. Do you remember, I called you yesterday morning?"

"I do." Now what?

"A Mrs. Digby came by just now, she said you told her to come and apologize."

"Yes, I did." Was a "thank you" coming up? I could hardly believe it.

Her voice rose the way it had before when we'd talked. "Well, I just wanted to tell you that that woman's crazy or something. What do you mean sending her here? The children are more frightened than before! Didn't you see there was something wrong with her when you talked to her? Are you blind—or just stupid? If I had your authority I'd put that creature away, she's as crazy as a bedbug . . ."

I cut into the high-pitched tirade. "Now, slow down, Mrs. Roberts. In the first place I didn't talk to the woman, I talked to her sister. What did she do that upset you so much?"

"Just one look at her is enough! She wears some kind of horrible black wig, a fright wig I'd call it, and she's plastered with make-up of the most obvious kind and her clothes are right out of World War Two."

"But what did she say? Do?"

"It wasn't what she did or said, it was the way she said and did it . . . oh, I wish my husband were here, but he's in New York on a business trip. I'm going to start looking for another house, I won't live near that woman . . ."

And then went on until I promised to talk to Mrs. Digby myself.

"What in the world was all that?" Brenda wanted to know.

I told her. She frowned thoughtfully. "Mrs. Clinton

Roberts? I think I met her in Newcomers' Club. She's a nervous little thing, hands like claws, thin as a rail. Her husband's always off somewhere, leaving her to run the show and I doubt that she's capable of it."

I pinched my lips together with thumb and forefinger. "That Miss Draggon's kind of an oddball and I guess her sister might be even more so. I'll drop by the next chance I get because I said I would. . . . What's on the TV this evening? Something other than another cop show, I hope. A comedy? I sure could use a good laugh."

Somebody was waiting for me in the station parking area on Monday morning, a guy wearing a ski jacket with a hood that was up, and his eyes were covered with sun goggles like skiers wear.

"Chief Severson?" He leaned over the car door, speaking politely through my half-open window.

"That's right." I rolled the window the rest of the way down. The sun was bright but the air was cold.

"I'm Rod Avery." He put a gloved hand out for me to shake.

I opened the car door and got out. "How are you feeling?" I asked.

"Okay. They let me out of the hospital Sunday." He just stood staring at me.

"What can I do for you?"

"I just wanted you to know I got your message."

"That's good. I meant it."

He grinned suddenly. "Oh, I know you did."

I waited but he just stood there. Finally I said, "See ya," and started into the station. When I got to the door I looked back. He was watching me. As I looked a gust of wind came along and blew the hood off so I could see stitches running up above his left ear—his head was totally shaved and the kid was as bald as a billiard ball.

A capacity crowd of Wellesley's best showed up at the Wellesley Club dinner meeting. It was held—where else —at the Harvard Club in Boston. Brenda and I drove in with Gary and Edith Lyons. Edith was a freckle-faced middle-aged lady who had obviously been a freckle-faced athlete at one time. Field hockey, I figured.

Superintendent of Schools Martin English, without his wife, got introduced to Brenda, as did Mr. and Mrs. Kendall Owens (I pegged her for Wellesley College, Class of, say, 1960) and Mr. and Mrs. Bill Sowerby (Wellesley High School, Class of 1965?). Alfreda Burke went out of her way to be nice to my wife, leading me to alter my first impression of Mrs. Burke—that from she's level-headed and fair-minded to she's level-headed, fair-minded and a good judge of people.

I was making polite conversation with my counterpart, Fire Chief Eddie O'Reilly, and his wife when Brenda nudged me and I glanced up to see Laurie Avery coming in with Chip Dawher and another woman who I took to be Mrs. Dawher. Mrs. Avery was, I conceded, a beautiful woman; her blond hair was piled atop her head and she wore what I would have described as a dress of many colors but which Brenda told me later was patchwork, mostly richly toned velvets and taffetas.

Entering just behind the Dawhers was Hugo Hix. Clutching his arm was a small, thin, birdlike woman. Brenda asked Mrs. O'Reilly "Is that Mrs. Hix?"

It was, replied Mrs. O'Reilly in careful tones. I watched as the newcomers mixed with the crowd. Hugo was beaming, shaking hands, slapping backs. Mrs. Hix smiled nervous little smiles and hung on to that arm for dear life. The Dawher trio, moving the other way, seemed to attract greetings while Hugo and wife had virtually to tug at sleeves to get attention.

We sat with Gary and Edith and the Dawhers, Mrs. Avery and a man named Talbot, who turned out to be Dr. Jeffrey Talbot of the Board of Health, an unpaid adviser to the town on matters of public health and an advocate of fluoridation of town water. "Don't even mention fluoridation," quipped Chip Dawher, "it's caused more conflict in this town than the Vietnam War."

Mrs. Burke, who would be chairman of the Board of

Selectmen come next March town meeting, spoke on "Less Taxes, Less Service?"

Gary and I sat in the front on the way home, the women in the back seat of the car. "Now I know what we are," Brenda chided, "middle-aged and middle-class, husbands up front, wives in the back."

"Gary always does this," Edith told us. "I don't mind, do you, Brenda? We can make catty remarks about all the women. Did you see that dress Rosemary Hix was wearing? I think she got it at a thrift shop."

"You know how close with a buck Hugo is," Gary spoke over his shoulder while expertly guiding the car onto the expressway. To me he added, "I've been told that when Hugo and Rosemary were married, he took her to Arizona on a honeymoon—courtesy of one of those real estate development deals where they fly you out, give you the heavy sales pitch and end up with your name on the dotted line."

"Did Hugo put his name on the dotted line?" Brenda wanted to know.

"Yes—and no. Or so the story goes. He signed, but when they got back to Wellesley he'd changed his mind. Thanks, but no thanks."

"When I heard about it," Edith put in, "I planned to write a book called *Memorable Honeymoons* and include that one. But I gave up the idea—could never find any others to go with it."

The Lyons dropped us at our door, we agreed we'd have to get together soon and, greeted by Mein Hair, who meowed that he wanted in, we found Frances Porter, our baby-sitting neighbor, watching Johnny Carson on the TV. She and Brenda chatted, I tucked her money into an envelope and slipped it into her coat pocket. The final chore was to see her home—which was, as I said, next door. Frances Porter had made her home with Mercy Bird ever since they'd met—and run into trouble—at a writer's colony last year. Mercy still wrote her mystery stories; Frances wrote poetry. They fought a good bit, we often heard them (especially in the summer when the windows were open), but they needed each other and we were relieved that Mercy was no longer alone. Well, not really alone. There had been, and still was, of course, Algernon, Mercy's Saint Bernard. Still, none of them was getting any younger.

"How is Mercy?" I asked Frances while she unlocked her front door.

"Deep in a thriller," Frances told me.

"I assumed so, I haven't seen her of late."

"Yes, I have to tread on eggs when she's in the throes. Good night, Knute. Get out of the doorway, Algernon, how can I get in with you standing there?"

Back on my front porch, I stood a moment. The night was clear and cold, stars were sharply bright in the black sky. Had I done the right thing in accepting the job of chief of police? I wasn't good at back-room politics, I wasn't the best at administration either, even though I was learning. I missed the personal contact with people, victims and/or culprits, even culprits. That, to me, was

real police work. Take this budget business . . . I opened
the door and went in. Brenda had already gone upstairs. I
went into the kitchen and took a beer out of the refrigerator.

"Knute? Are you coming up?"

"In a minute." I turned the TV back on. Carson was in-
terviewing a bosomy blonde who had written a book. I
finished the beer, turned the set off in the middle of a
commercial and climbed the stairs.

"Did you look in on Lief?" I asked Brenda.

"Uh-huh. Does that suit need to go to the cleaners?"

"I guess so."

"Leave it out then. But empty the pockets, please."

"Okay."

"You know, I feel kind of sorry for her."

"Who?"

"Rosemary Hix. People poke fun and he does sound like
an awful pill. But you could see that she adores him."

"She sure clings."

"Did you happen to see the look she gave Laurie
Avery?"

I snapped out the light. "Didn't notice."

"It was over in a second, I just happened to be looking.
If I ever saw hate in a woman's eyes—she positively
glared."

"Maybe she's jealous. I wonder . . . ?"

"Is there something going on there?"

"Uhm. Can't imagine Laurie Avery giving Hugo Hix
the time of day. . . . Still . . ."

"Still—what?"

"He did ask me to take it easy on her son."

Brenda sighed, moved close, I put my arm around her. "She's a stunning woman."

"Who? Laurie Avery?"

"Yes, of course." A pause. "Don't you think so?"

"I guess." I kissed her shoulder. "I prefer brunettes."

Brenda laughed. "Liar! When I met you, you had blonde girl friends in every Boston precinct."

"That was because brunettes were scarce. And many a blonde was a brunette to begin with." I touched her neck. It was a lovely curve, where Brenda's chin came down to smooth throat, to collarbone.

"And how do you know that, may I ask?"

"Hush. I have my own investigative methods."

"Have?"

"Had. If you don't shut up, we'll never get to sleep and I have budget problems on the morrow."

"Thank you," she whispered.

"For what?"

"For not allowing me to be jealous."

"Jealous? You? Of whom?"

"Laurie Avery and her ilk."

"Silly girl."

"That's just it. I'm not a girl anymore."

"Neither is she. Now shut up."

I hauled out my last year's copy of the town report to check on the format—the town report had to go along with the budget.

Annual Report of the Wellesley Police Department, photograph of the chief. God, that was an awful picture of me, I'd just as soon they left that out. Maybe they would. Wouldn't that cut down on the cost of the report? I made a note to ask Miss Miller to check with Sowerby.

Criminal cases prosecuted during the year? I had that figure somewhere but it wasn't right up to date. Motor vehicle cases prosecuted . . . escapees apprehended and returned to institutions . . . runaway children apprehended and turned over to parents . . . those arrested and turned over to other authorities . . . mental cases taken to institutions. . . . Homicides? None in the past twelve months.

Then, a breakdown on various duties: accidents, ambulance calls, bicycles registered, burglar alarms responded to (bank, store and residence), fire alarms responded to, radio messages, patrol-box duty calls, teletype messages, summonses delivered for other departments, vacant house inspection requests (so far 1,886), vacant house inspections (to date, 13,719), last (but not least), parking violations issued on streets and lots.

Then we came to revenue collected from parking meters and receipts from sale of xerox copies, photos, taxi badges, firearm identification cards, permits to carry firearms, bicycle registration.

Concluding with: the department consists of the chief of police, two lieutenants, three sergeants, forty-one patrolmen, one civilian clerk (Doddy Miller) and one custodian (Lester Ems).

All right. I was still putting it off. Down to business. The budget, under protection of persons and property.

We took in over $30,000—most of that came from salaries for special details, police hired by private individuals, clubs, businesses, etc. Weddings, big parties, charity affairs and so forth.

But—we spent: personal services (salaries), $554,109; expenses, $35,562; out-of-state travel, $200 (one lieutenant to Washington for an FBI seminar, we can cut that out maybe?). Capital outlay (police cruisers, equipment, repairs to building, maintenance) $17,000—total, well over $600,000, and the union was agitating for cost-of-living increases and additional paid vacations . . . damn, how did one cut to the bone?

"Chief Severson"—Miss Miller rapped and opened my door with one quick motion—"there's a Mrs. Digby to see you—I told her I wasn't sure you had the time . . ."

"Mrs. Digby?" Oh, yes, the Draggon woman's sister. I'd been planning to send one of the men out to see her—maybe this was better. "All right. I have a few minutes. Ask her to come in." (Putting off the budget again, eh, Knute?)

The family resemblance was certainly there, but she appeared to be taller and thinner. Her hair, curling carefully from beneath a fur hat, was jet black.

She had blue paint on her eyelids and the lashes above the blue eyes were stiff and black with mascara. Her color was high—make-up, I could tell—and her mouth was brightly painted. Somehow, even with all the camouflage, she looked older than her sister. But, then, Miss Draggon had said her sister was older.

Mrs. Digby wore a mink coat and high, black shiny boots. She wore pearl earrings and necklace and bracelets and rings. In brief, she was as different from her mousy, gingerbread-baking sister as she could be. "How do you do, Mrs. Digby. Please sit down."

She smiled widely. She had lipstick on her teeth. The Draggon resemblance was strongest in the eyes—those same bright blue eyes with the same childlike expression.

She said, "Florence was right. You are a handsome young man."

I passed that by as fast as possible. "Mrs. Roberts telephoned me, she said you came to call . . ."

The smile vanished, she leaned forward and tapped beringed fingers on my desk. "That woman is an inferior mother. All this permissiveness! I assure you that my father and mother raised us quite differently! Isn't there some department of cruelty to children you can report that woman to? Little children like that! Allowed to do as they please. How can a child know what is good for it? I've never had children, alas, but I've been a child and I remember—clearly—what it feels like to be a child." The red mouth split, showing the red teeth. "Sometimes I still feel like a child. Florence doesn't understand that."

This was building into one of those classic neighborhood feuds that every cop encounters early on in police work. The party of the first part runs to authority, complains about the party of the second part. The party of the second part refutes the complaint of the party of the first part by accusing said party of the first part of instigating the argument by impossible behavior, *ad infinitum*. It was like two little kids.

"Look, Mrs. Digby . . ."

"Please call me Veronica. It's a lovely name, don't you think? Veronica."

"Veronica, there's no law that forbids what you call permissiveness. I won't say that I agree or disagree with you, but there's no way that I or this department can change the character of Mrs. Roberts. The Society for the Prevention of Cruelty to Children, which is, I presume, the authority you refer to, has power only in cases of provable neglect or physical abuse. Now, I don't think you can contend that Mrs. Roberts is guilty of . . ."

She was an interrupter and a talker-at-length. "I'd say she was capable of anything, but you're right, I can't prove it and, heaven knows, I don't want to get involved. I don't have enough time for my own personal interests. And my health is not the best, unlike Florence, who has always been as healthy as a horse. She took after father, you see, he lived to be ninety-two, while I resemble my mother in temperament. Mother, poor dear, passed away at eighty-seven. Florence nursed them both, single-handedly, which shows you how healthy she is, because both were bedridden for some time and I, of course, was living in New York with George." She leaned forward intently. "No matter what anybody says about Florence, she must be given credit for that."

"Yes, I'm sure. Well . . ." I'd have to set up some sort

of signal with Miss Miller so that in the future she'd come in and rescue me from the likes of Mrs. Digby.

Perhaps she read my mind, because she abruptly stood up, clutching the big leather handbag with one hand and closing the fur coat with the other. "Thank you very much, Chief Severson. It's been a pleasure and I wish I could stay longer but I have so much to do."

I rose hurriedly. "Of course. And thank you, Mrs. Digby." I opened my office door for her, she swept out, bestowing, I presumed, lipsticked smiles. Miss Miller and Officer Hayes, on the desk, glanced curiously after her.

Now, I thought, back to the budget.

❖❖❖❖❖❖❖

Doddy, watching Mrs. Digby depart, thought again how very much Veronica Draggon had changed. She wouldn't have recognized her if she hadn't identified herself as Veronica Draggon Digby. But then, it had been years since she'd gone away and Doddy supposed that she herself had changed some. (Yes, when she looked in the mirror she saw salt and pepper hair and a thickening body. Funny how one could gaze at a mirror and see the person who had once been a girl and then a young woman, but no older, no older . . .)

Better call Mother to make sure everything was all right. This was the night Doddy did not go home after work (if everything was all right) because on two Mondays a months he attended the Quota Club dinner meetings and on the other two Mondays she went to the rehearsal of the Choral Society. ("I must have a little time off," she'd said to Dr. Ziggler, and the good doctor had agreed. "Get someone to come in one night a week," he'd suggested. "But who can I get?" had been Doddy's reply. Ask around, he'd said, and she had inquired of several people who had come once or maybe twice but then made excuses so finally she'd arranged that Clarice come on Mondays and stay through supper. It was expensive, but *necessary*.)

Tonight was Choral Society night and her custom was to have dinner at Howard Johnson's before going to the high school where the rehearsals were held. After the rehearsal, it was Doddy's habit to drive Isabel Terence home and Isabel invariably invited her in for coffee and a snack. It was always close to eleven o'clock when she got home, adding to the expense. Clarice made very good money cleaning other people's houses and minding other people's mothers, which was why Clarice had her own car, and a late model at that, to drive back to Dorchester in.

No matter, it was worth it. And she could afford it, with a little help from the gourmet counter at the supermarket and the wine alcove at the liquor store. One only lived once, didn't one? Yes, damn it. If she only had it to do over again . . . never mind.

She parked her car in the railroad parking lot so that she could walk down the street and look into the shop windows as she strolled the short distance to the restaurant. Christmas decorations were up already. Soon the stores would start staying open in the evenings, she loved to do her Christmas shopping then. Ever since she'd been a little girl she'd loved to go downtown at night, it was something about the lights, something exciting in the dark. . . .

Olken's store had ski clothes and equipment in its windows, Mr. Woods, the occulist (Or was he an optician? She never could get that straight.) had sprigs of holly arranged around glasses cases and frames. Doddy's eyes had been bothering her a bit of late, she hoped heartily that she wasn't due for bifocals, she hated the thought of them and, furthermore, eyeglasses had gotten so expensive, Marily Gwynn, a fellow Choral Society member, had told her that her new pair cost one hundred dollars. Imagine!

Woolworth's featured a lot of tinsel in its windows and along its ceiling and maybe even along its floor for all she knew. Doddy could remember clearly when Woolworth's was a five-and-dime, but nowadays five and ten dollars was more like it. Which made her think of taxes, real estate taxes, always going up, why didn't Hugo Hix spend some of his time trying to fix that?

Doddy waited for cars to pass and crossed Central Street, eager to look into the Marco Polo windows, which were clear glass top to bottom and showed the whole store full of lovely gifts and things for the home.

MacVan's had some handsome quilts in its display. She didn't go in there much, it was a small shop and almost impossible to shoplift from except when they were short-handed and somebody had to go downstairs to take an order for custom-made drapes and so forth, but even so, it wasn't safe and Doddy knew she had to play it safe. She pushed open the glass doors at Howard Johnson's and went in, hoping that there was a vacant booth, as she hated to eat at the counter. She saw one in the back and hurried toward it. She heard a voice speak her name from another booth and looked over to see Hugo Hix with some man she didn't know.

"Good evening, Hugo," she said coolly.

"How's your mother? Don't forget the Thanksgiving invitation."

"No, I won't." That man seemed to be everywhere, what was he doing here at Howard Johnson's when he had a wife and home to go to? She peeked over the top of her menu and saw that he wasn't eating but having coffee. He seemed to be carrying on quite a conversation with the strange man. Wonder what he wants from him, Doddy thought, and consulted the menu. She loved the fried clams, but what was the evening special . . . ?

This night the Choral Society concentrated on the "Hallelujah Chorus." They were to sing it at a Christmas festival in three weeks and chorus director Devon Smith assured the group that it definitely needed work.

Doddy sang soprano because she couldn't read music but she could carry a tune. Well, of course she knew perfectly well that the notes on the staff lines were e, g, b, d, f (every good boy does fine!) and that the notes on the staff spaces were f, a, c, e, it didn't take a genius to remember they spelled face, but she was unable to translate the notes into sound so she sang soprano because that was the melody and there were always more sopranos so you couldn't goof up so easily.

Isabel Terence sang soprano too. Isabel had once sung solos in her church choir, she'd told Doddy (told her often), but to Doddy's ear she sang flat. No matter, she was pleased to have Isabel Terence sit beside her at rehearsals. She would have had no chance ever to see Andy Terence again if she hadn't made friends with his wife. And it was important to Doddy to see Andy Terence.

She told herself sternly that she wasn't in love with her boss, pardon, ex-boss, or—if she was—it was a platonic love and had nothing at all to do with the physical aspect that caused so many people to run in silly circles. She loved the way he looked, big, a football player's build (well, maybe gone to seed, but an athlete for all that) and she loved the way he talked, the way his thick hair curled and the way his hazel eyes crinkled when he smiled, and she even loved the space between his two front teeth.

In contrast, Isabel was tall and thin to the point of

being scrawny and she had frown lines between her very pale blue eyes and her hair was mouse-colored. Doddy had often wondered what he ever saw in her other than the fact that Isabel's brother had been something big in the state police a few years back. No matter, they were indeed married (although childless) and had been for many years so that was that.

"Come in for a snack, won't you?" Isabel said as usual when Doddy drew her car up to the Terence walk.

"Well, I guess I can, if you're sure it's no bother. We won't disturb the Chief, will we?" In this, a conversation that had become ritual, Doddy always referred to Andy as Chief. She could never bring herself to use his first name in front of his wife. Nor could she call him Mr. Terence, they'd worked too long together for that. So Chief it had become, and he would, truly, always be Chief to her.

"Why, Doddy, I think he looks forward to your visits," Isabel told her, causing a feeling of intense pleasure throughout Doddy's body. "Since he's retired, he seldom sees anybody on the force, so many of his pals aren't retired, and they don't really have time to come visit." She patted Doddy's arm. "He's a little lonesome, I think. Feels like he's been put on the scrap heap. Not even Hugo Hix comes around anymore."

I'll bet, thought Doddy; what can Andy do for him now? She remembered once in school days Hugo had been running for office, but what office? Class treasurer, that was it, and he'd come around offering some sort of bribe—what? Tickets to the Community Playhouse—yes, that was it, he'd worked there nights at the time and Doddy remembered thinking, I'll bet he swiped those when the management wasn't looking. He didn't win the treasury post so it ended up that it didn't matter, but she'd thought at the time that Hugo Hix would be just the type to abscond with the class treasury and now she wondered fleetingly how he had ever gotten so popular as to be elected selectman of the town of Wellesley, another of life's mysteries.

Andy was watching TV and drinking beer. He did seem genuinely glad to see Doddy, even turned off the television to talk. When he offered her a can of beer she surprised herself by saying yes, "Singing is a thirsty business." She'd never before touched a drop of alcohol in front of Andy.

"How's it going?" he wanted to know while Isabel was busy in the kitchen. "How do you like this Severson boy?"

She studied her hands for a moment. She wanted to give her most honest answer. "He's unsure of himself, I think. Takes things slow and carefully. He gets kind of stiff-necked sometimes, but I think that's because he's uncertain." She smiled at Andy Terence. "He's got a long ways to go before he can be half the man you were." Once said, she was immediately appalled. Never had she ever said such a thing to the Chief.

He cleared his throat and drank from the beer can. When he lowered it she thought his face was pink. Had the Chief really blushed? The thought made Doddy's own face hot.

"What I saw of him, I liked," Andy said. "I think he'll come along." He grinned suddenly at Doddy, setting her heart racing. "Especially as long as he's got somebody like you to give him a hand."

"I'll do my level best, Chief," she promised. And when Isabel came back with the beer and pretzels, Doddy realized she didn't really need any alcohol tonight.

One unexpected responsibility that came with police chief territory was the annual Veterans' Day parade. It was Wellesley's only parade, a big deal as parades go, and I was duty-bound to march in it. I had to don my gold-buttoned, gold-braided dark blue chief's suit and lead a contingent of my men. The fire chief did likewise and led the thing off with fire engines sounding sirens. There were service units (Army, Navy, Air Force) and marching bands from all the high schools in and around the town; there were college bands, too, and bands from parochial schools and costumed bands who played professionally.

Furthermore, there were floats sponsored by various Wellesley businesses and organizations and, of course, there were the veterans' groups striding and/or struggling along, depending on which war the marcher was a veteran of.

And, naturally, the selectmen marched. Alfreda Burke and Kendall Owens and Hugo Hix stepped off the two-and a half-mile route as if they'd been doing it all their lives while I got sore feet the first time and anticipated more of the same this time.

Frankly, I felt like a damn fool.

Fire Chief Eddie O'Reilly echoed my sentiments as we awaited the start of the parade in the public works yard designated forming area. "At least we've got a good day," he said, looking up at the bright blue sky. "One year they had to postpone it, we had a regular northeaster."

"Wonder which is the lesser of the two evils," I murmured and Eddie laughed.

We got under way, more or less on time, and I assumed my best military stance, arms swinging, face front. Dennehy, to my right, kept making wisecracks, trying to break me up. The Wellesley Junior High band, just behind us, swung into "America, the Beautiful" every two or three blocks and I had to admit they didn't play too badly for little kids. I'd discovered it was easier to march to music.

Somebody yelled my name in front of the Town Hall so I turned to see who it was and spied Mercy Bird with her Saint Bernard, Algernon, straining at a leash fashioned from a rope. I didn't know what protocol called for so I gave Mercy a mock salute. Algernon made a lunge, trying to join me.

Brenda and Lief had said they'd be watching in the Square but so were a great many other people. We had to eyes-right at the reviewing stand; the selectmen were up there now I noted, along with other dignitaries. Just beyond was Doddy Miller standing behind an old lady in a chair. Her mother? I gave them a salute too.

At the end of Central Street we broke ranks near the college and I headed back for the Square looking for Brenda. We'd been invited to a luncheon at the Treadway Wellesley Inn so I was forced to go on wearing my uniform. I felt as though I was dressed for a costume party.

Ahead of me the parade was still coming through and people were wall to wall, and I still hadn't laid eyes on my wife and son. I came up behind Doddy and turned to avoid her—but she spotted me so I had to say hello.

She introduced me to her mother, a tiny old woman with enough make-up to put her in the clown contingent. Mrs. Miller fluttered her eyelashes and carried on like a girl, unlike her stolid, plain daughter. Glancing at Doddy, I thought she looked flushed. I saw Hugo behind her.

"I'll confess that I like parades," he was saying, "I get a big kick out of stepping down the street and waving to all my friends. Besides, it's very good for the town, you know. Gets everybody out, gets everybody together.

Creates an *esprit de corps*." He pronounced it like it's spelled.

"Have you seen my wife?" I asked him. "There are so many people, I haven't been able to spot her."

"I think she's over by the bank." It was Doddy who answered. I gave her a quick look—I didn't know she knew what Brenda looked like. "I met her at the Clothing Exchange," she added, almost defensively.

"Thanks very much." I smiled at Mrs. Miller. "A pleasure to meet you, ma'am."

"See you at the luncheon." Hugo beamed.

And so he made a point of seeing me at the luncheon. "I wonder if I could borrow your husband for a few minutes, Mrs. Severson?" He bowed to Brenda. "Town business, you know." He shook his head wisely.

"Of course." Brenda smiled politely.

"Daddy." Lief had been eying the dessert table and I'd promised to take him over to choose.

"I'll be right back," I assured him and followed Hugo over to a corner of the room. What now?

For once he seemed slightly ill at ease. "I don't know how to tell you this," he said, looking nervously around the room. "I don't want to tell you at all"—at last he eyed me—"but I've thought it over and there's nothing else I can do."

I stood waiting, but still he hedged. "I have a great deal of affection for her, to tell you the truth," he finally went on before he stopped again, making me wonder, Who in God's name is she?

"I tried to talk to her, but she simply denies the whole thing." He dropped his voice, close to whispering. "I'd take her word for it, but I can't. I saw her with my own eyes."

Out of the corner of one of my eyes I saw Brenda leading Lief to the cakes and puddings. "Hugo," I said, "you're not making yourself very clear."

He positively wriggled. "It's an unpleasant task . . . she seems to feel that I'm being vindictive and I'll grant you we had a small disagreement recently, but I would never accuse someone of . . ."

"Knute, have you met Admiral Kinally?" asked a voice behind me and I turned to see Kendall by the side of a frosty-looking gentleman in a fancier uniform than mine would ever be.

"No, sir." I put out my hand. "It's kind of you to join us for our parade," I told the admiral.

"Hell," said the admiral, "I grew up in Wellesley. Haven't been back in years. Town looks about the same. People have changed, though. Old Henry Prescott was chief in my day. Did you know Henry? No, I guess not, he'd be before your time."

"And this is my fellow selectman, Hugo Hix," Kendall said politely.

"I remember old Henry," Hugo spoke eagerly.

"He was an old son of a bitch," said the admiral. "Used to chase us boys through Nehoiden Golf Course for stealing golf balls. Only thing we were doing was fishing them out of the pond."

Hugo smiled reminiscently. "Yes, he was a tough old boy. I remember when . . ."

I interrupted. "Gentlemen, if you'll excuse me, I've deserted my wife and child . . ."

"Certainly, Knute." An expansive wave of the hand from Hugo. "I'll stop in at your office tomorrow and we'll continue our little discussion. Now, as I was saying, Admiral . . ."

❖❖❖❖❖❖❖❖

The following Friday morning I found one of my lieutenants, Harold Barnes, waiting for me when I got to the station. Barnes headed up the midnight to eight shift. He's a careful, ploddingly efficient police officer who takes everything pretty much in stride. That morning, however, he was actually pacing the corridor as I came in.

"I've just come from Mrs. Hugo Hix," he told me with little preamble. "She called in at daybreak. Hugo didn't come home last night."

"Come in, Barnes, sit down. Miss Miller, how about

some coffee?" Hugo had planned to come to see me, to tell me one of his little secrets, I recalled now. But he hadn't shown up, or if he had I hadn't been in. I'd check with Miss Miller when she brought in the coffee. "Mrs. Hix reported that Hugo didn't come home? When was this? How long has he been missing? When did she see him last?"

"He called about six-thirty and said he had an unexpected appointment, he'd be late. She hasn't heard from him since."

"Where did he call from?"

"She doesn't know. I got the idea he told her just as much as he had to and no more."

Miss Miller appeared with the coffee. "Has Hugo been in to see me lately?" I asked her. "He mentioned something at the parade luncheon about having something to tell me."

"Yes, Chief Severson. He came in one morning—let's see, not yesterday, the day before, I think. You'd gone down to the high school, if you recall . . . it was the day somebody pushed an old car into the brook . . ."

"Yes, I remember. What did he want? Did he leave a message?"

"He just asked for you and I told him you were out and he said he'd get back to you later, it wasn't important so I didn't bother to make a note." She looked apologetic. "I'm sorry. I didn't know you wanted to see him."

I almost said that I certainly didn't. I did say, "That's all right, Miss Miller. You know Mr. Hix. If it had been urgent, he'd have traced me down. He hinted that he had something to tell me about some woman, and now it seems that he didn't come home last night."

"Oh." Her face flushed as it had on parade day. "I think I might have an idea . . ."

"Yes?"

"He mentioned"—her face flamed now—"just in passing, we're old friends you know, that he wanted to talk to you about Mrs. Avery."

"Mrs. Avery? I see. Well, thank you very much, Miss Miller."

And as soon as she'd gone Barnes shifted his eyes, looking down at the floor. "Mrs. Hix—ah—wanted me to check at Mrs. Avery's."

"She did, did she? And did you check Mrs. Avery's?"

"I drove by. It was . . . maybe seven A.M. I didn't want to wake the woman that early if I didn't have to. The house was still dark, and I could see two cars in the garage because the doors were wide open. It was Mrs. Avery's car and another one, not Hugo's Cadillac. I came back and checked out the second license plate. It seems it's a new Audi she bought her son, it's registered in his name."

I picked up the phone and called the Hix residence. Mrs. Hix answered, her thin voice high, barely under control, I thought. I identified myself, but before I could ask a question she said:

"You've found him? Is he dead?"

"No, we haven't located him yet, Mrs. Hix, but it's early. He may have had car trouble, there's no reason yet to jump to any conclusions." Barnes had checked the local hospitals. "He's not in any nearby hospital, we know that. You have no idea where he was going?"

"He didn't say. I had an idea. I told the lieutenant. I guess he wasn't there." I couldn't tell from her tone whether she was relieved or disappointed.

"We'll get everybody on it, Mrs. Hix," I told her. "Check it out with surrounding towns. He's got a distinctive car, easy-to-remember license plates. The minute we know anything, we'll get back to you. And—if he should call or show up—you'll let us know, won't you?"

"Of course I will. I am not stupid." Her voice rasped, the way she said it gave me the idea she was refuting an often repeated charge.

I by-stepped that just as I had avoided the Avery reference. "Thank you, Mrs. Hix. Don't worry. We'll find him." When I'd hung up, I thought I was just as intimidated as Barnes. I should have asked her if he often stayed out all night. I was assuming he didn't, because she didn't wait very long to report him missing. But he could have had a pattern of being absent albeit with the proper excuses. If he didn't turn up right away, we'd have to open a can or two of worms. Damn the man!

I reached for the phone book to look up the Avery number but thought better of it. An in-person call might be more diplomatic. How did you tell one of the town's upper-echelon heroines that she was suspected of husband-stealing? Carefully, very carefully. Which is why I didn't tell Miss Miller where I was going, said only that I'd be back in half an hour.

The cars were still in the garage. The new Audi was a smart-looking dark blue job.

Rod Avery, clad in a woolly bathrobe, opened the door for me. "Well, well," he said in a toneless voice. "What have I done now?"

"I don't know. What have you done now?" I put a snap in my words.

He looked at me with pale green eyes, shrugged. "Is your mother up?" I asked. "I'd like to speak to her."

He stapped back from the door. "My mother rises at the crack of dawn," he told me. "Don't you know that's one of the good people rules—early to bed and early to rise?"

"Who is it, Rod?" called Laurie Avery from the back of the house.

"The long arm of the law," he answered. He grinned at me mirthlessly. "I read that someplace."

Mrs. Avery appeared at the end of the hall. She, too, wore a robe, a long, silky Chinesey thing in tones of blue and gold. "Chief Severson! Come on out to the kitchen. Won't you have some coffee?"

"Thanks." The kitchen was, as expected, large and beautifully appointed; it would have been sunny because of its many windows if it were not for the fact that it was a raw, cloudy day. Nonetheless, with its curtains printed in pink, green and white stripes and its marbled green formica counter tops and pink- and white-tile floor it was cheerful, a house-and-garden showplace.

Rod took my coat, dropped it on a chair and disappeared. I had the feeling he was listening someplace.

"Please sit down," Mrs. Avery invited, producing as she did so a cup of coffee from a machine with a tempered-glass pot at the bottom. "Sit down, and tell me quick that nothing is wrong." She smiled. "Then I can enjoy our visit."

"Thanks." I sat in a white captain's chair. What did I say next? I was just passing by and thought I'd drop in . . . ? "Hugo Hix appears to be missing. I just wondered if you'd seen him lately." So much for tact and diplomacy.

She stood looking at me, holding her own coffee cup in both hands. "No," she said slowly, softly, "I haven't seen Hugo since Monday night at the Wellesley Club."

I sipped. "Very good coffee."

She moved then, got herself another cupful. "Yes, isn't it? It's a new appliance, quite a good design I think. All these new conveniences, some of them are more trouble than they're worth." She sat down across from me. "When did Hugo—disappear?"

"Last night. Last heard of about six-thirty."

She frowned. "That's odd. Isn't it?" With lifted eyebrows, wide, clear eyes.

"His wife seems to think so."

"Rosemary suggested that you come and ask me where he was?"

I nodded.

"I see." She ducked her head to taste her coffee. She looked at me again. "Rosemary is a rather insecure person and, like many insecure people, she has a tendency toward unreasonable jealousy. Hugo and I are friends, we've worked together on several common causes. If Rosemary thinks our relationship is something more than that, she's quite mistaken."

I gave another nod. "It's just something we had to check out. You understand."

I got a lovely, friendly smile. "Of course I do." She flicked her eyelashes. "I have some good news. Rod has a part-time job. For the holidays. He's going to clerk at Olken's."

"That should keep him busy," I said.

She laughed. "Exactly. It's a good sign, don't you think? I had nothing to do with it. He got it on his own."

"Yes, I think it's a good sign. He came to see me, you know. Right after he got out of the hospital."

"Oh?" She hadn't known. "What did he want?"

"I'm not sure. To thank me, I guess." I'd drained my cup, pushed back my chair. "Thank you, Mrs. Avery. Sorry to bother you."

"Don't you think you might call me Laurie?" She laughed softly. "Maybe then I wouldn't get a sinking feeling in my stomach every time you ring the doorbell."

I picked up my coat, put it on. Several things came to

mind, but all I said was, "Thank you for the coffee. Tell Rod I wish him good luck."

I found my own way out.

Hugo Hix's house was about the same vintage as 20 Howe Street where Brenda and I lived, but it had been modernized. Wooden clapboards had been replaced with aluminum siding, the macadam surface of the driveway was not black top but green top, colored to match the grass of the summer.

The yew bushes along the front were safe in A-shaped wooden frames, not a leaf—well, maybe a few—marred the closely cut lawn. Hugo the gardener? I hadn't heard that, but maybe he was.

The house was white with green aluminum blinds. In the center of each blind and on the front storm door was an H. I walked up cleanly swept cement steps and pushed the doorbell button. Chimes. What else?

"Any news?" asked Rosemary Hix upon opening the door. She wore a black turtleneck jersey and black polyester pants. She looked like a smooth stick of licorice.

"I'm afraid not."

"Come in." Black was an unfortunate color for her skin, hair and eyes. The birdlike image returned. Perhaps it was because she wore no make-up, but she looked at least five years older to me.

She led me down a hallway papered with white ivy on pale green. She turned left into a small room, not the living room, preciously paneled in shellacked knotty pine, containing brown leatherette sofa and chairs, two olive-green filing cabinets and a glass-fronted bookcase. A modern Danish-style desk held center stage. Its drawers were only partially closed, as though someone had been rummaging through it. The long narrow center drawer had a brass hole where a key should go. It was scarred and so was the wood above it. "I jimmied it open," explained Rosemary Hix. "He has the keys."

I didn't touch the desk but asked, "What did you find?"

She laughed, a squeaky kind of titter. "The checkbook, at least I found the checkbook. It's in his name, naturally. But they'll let me write checks on it, won't they? I am his wife."

The way she said "I am his wife" reminded me of Richard Nixon proclaiming "I am the President." If he ever actually said those words. Comics miming him did.

"May we sit down, Mrs. Hix?" I asked quietly. This one was on the verge.

"Yes. Of course. Not that chair. That's Hugo's. Won't you take your coat off? You'll be warm."

I unbuttoned it, looked for a place to put it (not, by God, on Hugo's throne), finally folded it over the back of the chair she'd chosen for me. Mrs. Hix sat—collapsed is a better word—on the fat-cushioned sofa.

"You sound as though you don't expect him to return," I began cautiously.

"I've thought and thought," she said after a moment. "He's either dead or—he's gone forever. Maybe to Arizona."

"Arizona?"

"Yes, we own a piece of land there. It's in his name. Naturally." She took a bite of fingernail.

I remembered now the story about the honeymoon. "Why would he go to Arizona—without a word?"

Her eyes were like beige seedless raisins. "I don't know. To get away."

"Away from what?" Hugo was a manufacturer's representative, clad metals, computer parts, bits and pieces that the average man wouldn't know what to do with. Had he possibly absconded with some firm's money? His office was in Wayne Park. We'd checked there, of course. His secretary, a Miss Keenan, seemed as baffled as the rest of us.

"I don't know—from what? How would I know? He never told me anything."

We'd better begin at the beginning. "Yesterday, when he called, at about six-thirty you said . . . ?"

"Yes. I already had dinner in the oven. Roast beef. It was ready to come out at six-forty, I had timed it perfectly. Hugo liked it just so, not too rare, not too well done."

"This was your normal dinner hour, then? Six-thirty or thereabouts?"

"Six-forty, precisely. Hugo said that people who ate before six-thirty were gauche—it was a word he learned recently. And, he said, people who ate later, eight o'clock maybe, were decadent. Drunkards, he said. Most of them. Hugo doesn't drink."

"In that case, if he called at six-thirty, he'd left it until the last moment. As though it were an emergency?"

She smiled slyly. "Either that, or he meant me to think so."

"If he weren't going to be home to dinner, did he usually call earlier?"

She nodded positively. "Oh yes. Do you know what roasts cost these days?" She looked downcast. "It's ruined."

"Did he ever stay out all night before?"

"Only when he was out of town. On business. Or a convention. Hugo loved conventions."

"Now, when he called, what exactly did he say?"

She rolled her eyes ceilingward. "He said, 'Rosemary, something's come up. I'm going to be a little late.' And I said, 'But Hugo,' only he didn't let me finish the sentence —he never did, well, hardly ever. He said, 'I can't help it. I shouldn't be long. I'll be home as soon as I can.' And I said, 'The roast!' but he'd hung up and I thought later that maybe he didn't remember we were having roast, he didn't always listen to me, and I'm pretty sure if he'd remembered he would have put it off to another night."

"Did you hear any background noises?"

"What do you mean?"

"Over the telephone. Cars passing? Music? Air conditioning? Voices? Any sounds?"

Another glance ceilingward. "I don't think so. Let me think." She seemed to have gone into a kind of trance. Finally, she shook her head. "Nothing. He was probably in his office."

"What makes you think that?"

"It's soundproofed."

"His secretary left at five-thirty and she said he was still at his desk. You could be right. He didn't give any hint at all about the nature of the emergency?"

"I told you. No." She sounded petulant.

I said mildly, "I'm only trying to help. Sometimes we forget a detail that we remember later. We've got a Telex out on his car, every department in the Commonwealth is on the lookout. The moment we hear any news, we'll let you know, Mrs. Hix. In the meantime"—I stood up, collected my coat—"try not to worry too much. I know that's easy to say . . ."

Rosemary Hix looked back at the ceiling, I couldn't help looking too; was there something fascinating up there? No, just an ordinary plastered ceiling. I said goodbye and was almost out the door when she said, "He won't be back so I've stopped worrying."

I glanced back at her, she was still staring at something up there, wherever up there was. "Who's your family doctor, Mrs. Hix?"

"Why?"

"Perhaps he could give you something, a tranquilizer, something."

She gave me a straight look then for the first time, a cold look. "If I need a doctor, I'll call one."

I nodded encouragingly. The lady was one mixed-up

lady, I thought. When I left, I asked her, "Will you be all right?"

She seemed to pull herself together some and nodded. "We'll find him," I said. She didn't respond to that.

I'd learned the technique of delegating authority, but I hadn't yet found the handle on the follow-through. I called in Blakely and Thorne, who had earned detective ratings under Terence and seemed to work well enough on house breaks and shopliftings. Nevertheless, I wasn't completely sold on their abilities now. Finding Hugo Hix was priority number one. I spelled that out carefully.

"There are three possibilities we have to take into account. One, he could have gone off on his own; two, he's been involved in an accident; three, he's been abducted."

Blakely, the elder of the two, wrinkled his prelined forehead. "Who'd want to abduct Hugo?"

I was patient. "I know it sounds unlikely, but he could have been kidnaped. Just because there's been no ransom note doesn't mean we can rule that out." I almost wished we'd get one. A ransom note would give us something to work with.

Thorne ran a hand over his close-cropped hair. "If there's been an accident, somebody should have heard."

"Unless it happened in some out of the way place where the car hasn't been spotted."

"I figure he took off on his own." Blakely looked stolidly at me through his bifocals.

"Got any idea why?" I asked.

He shrugged. "Hugo's a shrewd little bastard. Could be

a dozen reasons. Maybe he stole money. Maybe it's a dame. An insurance racket? I wouldn't put anything past Hugo." He sounded almost admiring.

"Insurance. Yes, check that. Bank accounts. He must have some kind of bookkeeping system at his office. Debts, too. Find out what kind of financial shape he was in."

Thorne pulled at his upper lip with two fingers. "Can't do a thing on an abduction angle, not unless we get something to go on. If somebody wanted to grab Hugo . . ." He shrugged. "Could be anybody. From anywhere."

"There'd have to be some Wellesley connection. Outside of this town, his is not exactly a household name."

"I don't know." Blakely's voice matched his looks, heavy and slow. "He's done a lot in politics, he helped get the governor elected and he's some kind of big wheel in the state selectmen's association. Political snatches are big things these days."

I nodded. Even though I didn't believe that anyone outside the town could take Hugo seriously. A cocklebur attached to a pant cuff, that was Hugo. Yet, he could raise my hackles pretty high. So, in this day of the loose nut, nothing's impossible.

Thorne outlined all the obvious moves in case of accident. I nodded as though he'd said something smart.

Blakely ran over a list of places to look for a hint that Hugo'd grabbed money—any money—and run. I nodded some more.

"What about a woman?" Thorne leered.

"The word is that Hugo and that Mrs. Avery are pretty chummy." Blakely blinked at me.

"I've talked to her, she's not out of the picture. I don't think Hugo was . . . her type, but . . ." I got off the direct subject of Laurie Avery as soon as I could. "She's got a son who could be bad news. You can look into that, only . . . don't lean on him." Now, why did I say that? The Avery virus settling in? No, it was because I sensed Rod Avery was walking some kind of tightrope.

"We can talk to some of the Avery neighbors," Thorne suggested, as though he'd come up with a bright idea.

I nodded. "Talk to the Hix neighbors, too."

Blakely blinked once more. "You mean, you got some ideas about Rosemary Hix?"

I nodded again.

They nodded back.

"And then there's Hugo's secretary. Miss Keenan."

More nods. Blakely allowed wisely, "You can never tell about secretaries."

I wished he'd winked when he said that. That was all we needed to be winkin', blinkin' and nod. I was beginning to feel like one of those clown toys with a round bottom. I sent them on their way.

When they'd left, I knew why they'd annoyed me so. I wanted to be out checking on Hugo Hix myself rather than sitting there, depending on somebody else.

That's what I mean about not finding the handle on the

follow-through. I couldn't get over the idea that I could do a better job than any man on my force.

Yes, I know all they say about pride and falls.

❖❖❖❖❖❖❖

Blakely and Thorne brought back what answers they could. Insurance coverage, $20,000 life. Not exactly a fortune. Nary a financial problem. Hugo had a healthy checking account, an even healthier savings account, A-number-one credit. According to a local bank official, Hugo was careful with his money. Furthermore, there'd been no unusual withdrawals, at least in the past few months, so unless Hugo was picking up cash from some unknown source, it appeared that he hadn't taken off with a pocket full of bread.

Cash from an unknown source? I got to thinking about that. He was a selectman, that meant he was a source of power and sources of power had had their pots sweetened in probably every city in the world. But in Wellesley? I'd heard the opposite. When I'd begun to consider the police chief post, I'd been assured that the town was more graft-free than most. Dennehy had sworn that nobody was really on the take.

Still—men didn't vanish, here one minute, gone the next, without reason. And how had Hugo fattened that savings account in these roughish times? I wouldn't want to bet a bundle on Hugo refusing a small tangible expression of appreciation from some of those whose names and problems he listed on the back of grocery tapes. Who had he mentioned on his last visit? I tried to recall. Mrs. Avery. I thought I knew the kind of favors he wanted from her. Some guy with a dog. Some guy who lived near Morse's Pond. I checked the log. Stanley Beech, that was the name. A boy named Homer Aborn had been bitten by Beech's dog. I decided to pay a courtesy call on Stanley Beech. I'd do that right after I followed up a long shot in Arizona. Mrs. Hix had collected her thoughts and came up with the name of the development where she and Hugo had spent their honeymoon. It was in a settlement I'd never heard of outside of Tucson. I asked Miss Miller to get long-distance information and connect me person to person with the head man at the nearest law enforcement agency. She produced a state police lieutenant named Harley. Lieutenant Harley sounded a little like John Wayne.

I told him I was looking for a missing person, described Hugo, filled Harley in on the details. He let me go all through that and he told me the development had gone bust, but, he said, he'd file the missing-person data just in case and how was the weather up my way, it was sunny and warm in Tucson, the air was as clear as air should be in God's country.

I cut him short, and regretted the cost of the phone call, since here I was trying to keep the cost of the department budget down. I went out to my car, noticed that it was raw and cloudy in this part of God's country and made my way out to Stonecleve Road. Stonecleve was one of three or four narrow, nonconformist streets that led to Morse's Pond from the back side. The houses in the area had once been summer camps, now they were year-round residences but the summer-camp stamp was still in evidence here and there. Beech's place was one of those heres and theres; the front porch had been closed in with windowed panels. As I started up the steps, I heard the deep, businesslike barking of a big dog.

When the door opened, I saw a wispy little man clinging to the collar of a Great Dane; neither seemed pleased to see me. When I told Beech, loudly, who I was, he shouted over the noise of the Great Dane, "Wait till I put him in the kitchen." He shut the door in my face, left me standing on the porch getting chilled.

Finally he returned, breathing hard, and let me in. The room I entered was small and cluttered. I gave up trying to identify all the smells.

Beech started babbling about the dog; he needed a watch dog, he said, kids had gone crazy, no telling what they'd do anymore and the pond was a natural attraction. I cut him off with a few words about how the dog officer and the selectmen's office handled dog complaints, I was here on another matter.

"Oh?" Beech was maybe fifty–fifty-five; his hair was

dun-colored and thin, and his teeth could have used a good cleaning.

I told him about Hugo disappearing. He'd heard about that, but why was I coming to him? The dog, behind a door, began to bark again. He began to scratch at the panels. I hoped it was a solid door.

"I'm checking with the people who saw Hugo last week. He was here, wasn't he?"

Beech narrowed little pale eyes. "Naw. I talked to him on the telephone. I've known Hugo most of my life, I didn't have to draw him a picture."

"Did you talk about anything else other than the problem with your dog?"

"Naw. I told him the problem. He said he'd see what he could do. Many's the time over the years Hugo's handled little things for me, Hugo's a good friend to the little guy, you know." That was about the first kind word I'd heard about Hugo. "What do you reckon has happened to him?"

"Did you ever do any favors for Hugo in return?" I asked back. I had to speak loudly to be heard over the dog.

"What the hell do you mean?" Beech's tone was belligerent.

"I mean, did you buy him presents? Give him money?"

"Hah!" Beech's smile was a sneer, maybe not at me but at somebody. "What would I use for dough? Didn't you know, I'm on the dole, buster. The last of the Beeches taking welfare from the town. My old man's whirling in his grave. Serves him right, the bastard."

The dog roared, seemed about to break the door down. I told Beech he'd better keep that animal restrained and I got out of there. Between the noise and the strange odors, I was getting a headache.

Russell Road was more or less right around the corner, so I figured as long as I was in the neighborhood I might as well call on the Aborns.

Homer was at school, his mother told me. Father Aborn was at work. Mrs. Aborn was a comfortable-looking, middle-aged housewife type and, for a change, a little impressed at receiving a visit from the chief of police.

We talked about Beech's dog. She seemed pretty sensible about the matter. "One of the selectmen called my husband and tried to tell Jeff—that's my husband—that Homer had been trespassing on the Beech property. Jeff told him that Homer was delivering papers and that he certainly wouldn't deliver any more papers to Mr. Beech. The man backed down then, Jeff said, and told Jeff that Beech was a sad case and he didn't want him in a lot of trouble. Jeff said, well, maybe so, but my boy's been bitten. Anyway Jeff talked to another selectman, the lady, Mrs. Burke? She assured him the dog would be restrained and our insurance company paid for the doctor and Homer's all right so I guess that's that. Some of our friends said sue and Jeff said you can't get blood out of a turnip. Homer's okay, that's what's important to us, that and the dog's being tied so he can't bite somebody else. He is tied up, isn't he?"

"Beech is keeping him in the house." I made a mental note to make certain that animal was kept under control.

"This selectman who called your husband, was it Hugo Hix?"

It was, of course.

"Did they talk about anything else other than the dog incident?"

She looked puzzled. "No. I know they didn't. I picked up the extension phone and listened in. Why do you ask?"

"Mr. Hix has disappeared." I saw her tense up. "I'm just talking to anyone Hugo had business with during that time . . ." This was a useless interview, too, I'd suspected that before I came.

"I never laid eyes on the man that I know of, Jeff neither. We've only lived here two years, two years and three months . . ."

"I see. Well, thank you, thank you very much . . ."

Her curiosity overcame her resentment. "He's disappeared? Just like that? Isn't that strange? You don't suppose it was the Mafia or anything like that, do you?"

I blinked. "The Mafia?"

"We used to live in Rhode Island and Jeff said the Mafia ran everything in the town we lived in . . ."

I shook my head. "So far as I know, Mr. Hix had no connection at all with any such organization." Now there was a far-out-in-left-field idea. I couldn't imagine Hugo vis-à-vis the Godfather. Hugo was a little godfather of sorts himself.

"Maybe he killed himself. On one of the TV stories I watch, Larry, he was Jennifer's husband, Larry wanted Jennifer to get his insurance money so he didn't want his death to look like suicide so he planned it very carefully . . ."

"Anything is possible," I told her as I reached for the doorknob behind me, "but we have no evidence to indicate that. Thank you very much, Mrs. Aborn."

And as I shut the door behind me, I heard her saying, "Could it have been drugs? A drug ring . . . ?"

I took a deep breath once in my car. Driving back to the station, I found myself feeling sorry for Hugo Hix. All of those people he listed under "things to do for," were they knocking down doors at the police station trying to help? No. Poor old Hugo . . .

There had to be some quirk in Hugo's character that led to his disappearance, but I'd be damned if I could pick it out. He was a do-gooder, a nose-poker-inner, a tightwad, a household tyrant male chauvinst-style . . .

Back to square one. Rosemary Hix? Laurie Avery? Laurie's son? Eenie, Meenie, Minie—as for Moe, Hugo, where did you go?

❖❖❖❖❖❖❖❖

Hugo's Cadillac was found two days later and it was found only then because we'd had an unexpected early snowstorm that brought us eight inches of white stuff and caught a lot of people without their snow tires. It was a freak storm, usually our snowy months are January and February, occasionally December and March, but this early November storm dropped enough snow to bring out the snow plows and foul up commuter traffic but good.

At the railroad station on Route 128, some six or seven miles from Wellesley, crews dug out a clutch of snow-covered commuters' cars, and while they were digging, a state police cruiser wheeled in to check on something else and there, among the vehicles left by Amtrak passengers, was Hugo Hix's Cadillac. You couldn't miss it, once you knew where to look. Hugo had chosen as his vanity plate HUGOH.

The car was locked, but on the driver's side only, and the keys were in the ignition. Hugo's prints were all over the driving area, and an assortment of fingerprints was found on the passenger side of the front seat. The state police lab, at my request, did a thorough job on the Caddy. They found hairs—brown, black, gray, red, blond —which were labeled and saved for evidence, should we need evidence. The back-seat area of the car was pretty clean but from the front floor they identified various foreign matter including clayey soil, sand, several strands of dried grass, a couple of decimated maple leaves, a crumpled Marlboro cigarette pack and a book of matches advertising a correspondence course.

I reported to Mrs. Hix by telephone. "He could have taken the train into Boston or he could have gone south to New York. I've notified Rhode Island, Connecticut and

New York authorities. We can't be certain how long the car was there—we know only that it was parked there before it snowed. The Cadillac is here at the station. Do you want to use it? I can have a man bring it over."

"I don't drive." Mrs. Hix sounded like a child over the telephone. "I never learned. I suppose you'd better put it in our garage, eventually I'll have to sell it . . ."

"Don't give up hope." I started to add, he's got to turn up somewhere, sometime, but I knew that many missing-person files remained open-ended and I didn't want to lie to her, she had enough problems.

If he skipped, he hadn't taken much money, at least no big chunks of missing cash. He'd cashed his usual fifty dollar check at the main branch of the South Shore National two days before he disappeared. How far could you get on fifty bucks these days?

I met with the other two selectmen. Mrs. Burke wondered if I'd checked with Hugo's doctor to see if he had a medical history that might shed some light on the disappearance.

"Yes, ma'am, I checked. Dr. Appleby says Hugo was sound as a bell." I grinned. "Dr. Appleby enjoys old clichés." Dr. Appleby had also said that Rosemary Hix was probably beginning to travel the menopause route. She remained my best suspect, but I couldn't get around the testimony of neighbors. Rosemary had been home that evening, she'd been seen moving inside and outside the house at various times by various people throughout that afternoon and evening. That left me with a lone possibility—Rosemary might have found someone willing to get Hugo out of her hair. But who? And how? I didn't spell any of this out to the selectmen, my responses to their questions were negative enough as it was. To everything they asked me, I'd had to answer no and if they asked me if Rosemary was behaving like a woman who'd had her husband murdered, I'd have to answer no again. She was behaving like a mixed-up woman in shock, from all reports.

Kendall Owens had been thinking. "It seems he either took the train or got into another car."

"Or set off on foot. Or hitchhiked. Or . . ." I made a "who-knows?" gesture.

Mrs. Burke frowned. "It's totally out of character."

"I agree," Owens seconded her comment, and I thought, You're so right, Alfreda, that's the crux of the problem. The whole disappearance bit is out of character.

"*Cherchez la femme?*" asked Sowerby from the other side of the table where he was taking notes. Whenever I saw Sowerby at Town Hall he was taking notes.

I wasn't sure how far to go on that line. "If he was playing games with anyone, he kept it pretty quiet."

"Laurie Avery?" asked Mrs. Burke. Mrs. Burke was a spade-caller.

I shook my head. "I can't swear to the nature of their relationship, but she knows nothing about his vanishing act as far as I can tell." I shrugged. "Of course, she could be a damned—pardon—good actress."

Sowerby grunted and Owens sighed. "We're in a very

strange position. Of course, Alfreda and I make up a majority of the board so long as we're both available for meetings, but I've planned to go skiing in Colorado between Christmas and New Year's and Alfreda's been looking forward to a cruise in January. What if he doesn't show up by then?"

"Wait a few days, we're doing our best. In the meantime, have you talked to Gary Lyons?"

"Town counsel is studying the ramifications. With the election set for March—we may have to call a special election—only how can we if we don't know, really, if he's alive or dead?"

"Is there no precedent for appointing an acting third member of the board?" Alfreda wanted to know.

"That's one of the things Gary is looking into." Owens sighed again.

And, inwardly, so did I. Where the devil was this gregarious, gossipy, fingers-in-every-pie guy? As Mrs. Burke said, this slick disappearance was totally out of character.

"Report to us daily, would you, please?" asked Mrs. Burke.

"Yes, of course." At the door I paused. "If Hugo doesn't turn up, who do you think would replace him as selectman?"

Kendall raised his eyebrows. "We still haven't decided who we're backing—unless it would be Frederick Collins."

"Frederick always runs against Hugo," Mrs. Burke explained. "He always loses but he always runs. Only against Hugo."

"That's interesting," I said. "I'll get back to you."

Frederick (never Fred) Collins, I discovered, was, more formally, Frederick Alexander Collins, III. From Frederick Alexander Collins, II, he had inherited an old Federal-type Colonial on Hundreds Road and a block of buildings in Wellesley Square. Dennehy told me (I always queried Dennehy if I could because I didn't mind looking stupid in front of him) that Frederick Collins was considered a lightweight. "He's as soft as a grape," was the way Dennehy put it. "He must be nearly sixty now, my father used to work for his father back in the old days when the Collins house was an 'estate.' According to my old man, Fred the Third was a real cross to bear, kicked out of all the best prep schools, and they wouldn't take him in the service in World War Two when they were taking almost anybody. He's a real creep."

I told him the reason for my curiosity. He replied, "With Fred the Third, I'd believe anything, except that I don't think he's smart enough to pull it off. Still, you never know."

I went to see Frederick Alexander Collins, III. The house was huge, three stories tall, with four chimneys sticking up above the peaked roof. It needed painting, a couple of slats were missing here and there along the porch railing, old venetian blinds were pulled down at the street windows.

The door had a bell and a knocker. The bell didn't sound so I worked the knocker and after a few minutes and a couple more raps of the knocker the door opened.

The man who stood in the doorway was big and shaggy. His hair, gun-metal gray, was frizzy-curly and stood out around his head like an Afro. He had small pale eyes and a good-sized nose, and perched near the end of it was a pair of half glasses. His clothes hadn't seen a pressing in many a day, and beneath his gray suit jacket he wore a brown sweater decorated with moth holes. "Mr. Collins?" I asked.

"I am. Who are you?"

"Chief Severson." That rang no bells. "Chief of Police Severson."

"What town?"

"Wellesley."

"What happened to Terence?"

"He retired a year and a half ago." He had very good teeth, which I didn't think were false; he was the end result of a series of expensive dentists, I'd bet.

"That so? Hadn't heard it. Too busy. What do you want?"

"If I could talk to you for a few minutes?"

"I'm a very busy man. Very busy indeed. I hate to interrupt my work."

I wondered what he was working at, made a guess: stuffing dead animals? Sticking pins in butterflies? "It's about Hugo Hix."

He pushed the half glasses up on his nose, peered through them at me. "Come in," he said, and moved aside.

The wide front hall, of graceful proportions, was

jammed with furniture. Instead of one Victorian hatrack, there were three; at least half a dozen umbrella stands were lined up against one wall; across from them stood a curio cabinet where every inch of space was filled with sea shells. Next to that was an oriental chest painted black and accented with gold and inlaid mother of pearl. On its top was a big brass pot with dead fern fronds hanging out of it. And there was a lot more I didn't take in because I was following Fred the Third into a study where walls were lined with books and where more books were stacked on chairs, on the floor, everywhere except on the top of a large mahogany desk, which looked nude, containing, as it did, a green blotter, a pad of graph paper, six neatly sharpened pencils and a thin book.

"Crosswords," said Frederick Collins, noting my glance. "I create crossword puzzles."

"Oh, I see. That must be—difficult."

"Very simple when one knows how. What's this about Hugo Hix?"

He hadn't asked me to sit down and all the chairs and a couch were book-laden so I stood and fenced, "When did you see him last?"

The glasses had slipped down on his nose once again. He pushed them back, looked through them, said, "Why?"

"He's disappeared."

Now he removed the glasses, held them in his hand, waved them back and forth. "You think I did away with dear Hugo?" He smiled. The teeth were perfect. Maybe they weren't his, but they looked so natural.

"Somebody suggested you didn't care much for him."

"Ready?" Still smiling. "That's an understatement if I ever heard one."

"In that case, when did you see him last?"

"I think you'd better sit down. Here." And he removed a dozen or so volumes from a chair, piled them atop another pile on another chair. A couple fell off. He paid no attention.

I unbuttoned my coat, decided not to remove it—it was cool, if not cold, in this room. I sat and Collins did likewise at the chair at the desk.

"Now." With the glasses laid down on the desk, he clasped his hands over one knee. "Tell me all about it. I've heard rumors, of course. That he'd run off with the Avery woman. Didn't believe that at all. Hugo is not the romantic type."

Patiently: "You haven't said when you saw him last."

Raised eyebrows: "At the Wellesley Club, of course."

"Oh? I didn't see you there."

"You didn't know me, did you? So you wouldn't have noticed me. I was there. Came in late."

That might explain it, I would have noticed him, all right.

"When did he disappear?" asked Fred the Third.

"The next evening. Sometime after six-thirty P.M."

"Ah!" The smile returned. "In that case, I have an alibi. I stayed in Boston after the Wellesley Club, at the Copley

Plaza if you care to check. I had an appointment for the next day. With my crossword editor. He came from Chicago and we were together that whole day and night, he left the next. You can check that out, too. I am . . ." He paused. "Give me an eight-letter word for blameless."

"Innocent."

"Correct."

"Have you any theories? Why should he suddenly vanish?"

"Have you checked his accounts? If Hugo vanished, he must have taken every loose cent in sight along."

"He didn't. Nothing's out of order, according to his secretary."

"Really? Strange. If that's true, then it must have indeed been foul play." A wide smile. "I must admit I'm flattered. Am I the first you thought of?"

"After the ladies."

"The ladies? Mrs. Avery and . . . ?"

"Mrs. Hix."

He clapped his hands. "Marvelous. Of course. You are a bright policeman. Not the proper term—a three-letter word for policeman?"

"Cop?"

"Pig? That's in bad taste, isn't it? Tec? A four-letter word, flic. A six-letter word, shamus. A twelve-letter word, investigator or interrogator. I'm sorry I can't help you, Chief Terence."

"Severson."

"Spell it."

I did. He wrote it down with one of the pencils and peered up at me. "If you want my opinion, I vote for Rosemary Hix. She was Rosemary Vale, you know. Her father was a builder, and he thought the sun rose and set in his Rosemary, she was his only child. He spoiled her pretty good, I'll bet he's been turning in his grave ever since she married Hugo."

"How long have they been married?"

Frederick squinted. "Let's see—Vincent Vale died some ten–twelve years ago, I'd say. Left Rosemary on her own —her mother had passed away when she was a teen-ager. Well, no sooner had old Vincent been put underground, six months at the most, Rosemary became Mrs. Hugo Hix. There was some talk about so soon by some and then there were some romantics who called it a whirlwind romance. I called it Hugo setting his sights, then—bam! Rosemary's inheritance was what he wanted. First thing he did was buy a Cadillac." He grinned. "Not a new one, of course. Hugo wouldn't part with that much money all at once, no matter how much he had in his sock."

"She is wealthy, then? She seems—unpretentious."

"Oh, Rosemary's got a business head on her shoulders, don't let anybody tell you otherwise. She'll make out all right, now that she's rid of Hugo. If she is rid of Hugo, which I earnestly hope. . . . I've known him all my life and disliked him all my life. He's a conniving hypocrite— big mouth, small brain. Can't stand to see the town run by that weasel. Upstart, too. His family came here after the Depression, my family's been here since the town was

incorporated, my grandfather and my father were selectmen in their day. You'd think that would count for something and it used to. But times have changed, I'll tell you.
They don't know the value of the name Collins. If they
vote at all, they vote for a Hugo Hix because he gets his
picture in the paper every chance he gets." He glared at
me as though it were my fault. "Disgusting."

Unadulterated jealousy showed in his eyes. He'd found
his self-failure scapegoat in Hugo. I said slowly, "Well,
maybe it's like you said and you're rid of him for good."

"Good riddance!" His face changed, resumed its amia-
ble, almost foolish, expression. "But don't misunderstand
me. I wouldn't soil my hands with him. Rosemary, well, it
can't have been all peaches and cream living with Hugo.
Or, if not Rosemary, well, maybe he found something better. Maybe he's sitting on a pile of money somewhere
laughing at us all." He played with the pencils on his
desk. "I wonder, if he doesn't show up, if I'll be appointed
acting selectman until the next election? The way it
works with town meeting members, when one leaves
town or dies, they name the highest vote getter among
the losers. That would be me. Nobody else has run
against him the last two times." He glanced up. He really
wanted that appointment.

"I don't know," I told him, and got ready to go.

"I believe I'll call the town clerk and see if she knows."

I thanked him for his courtesy and left him dialing his
telephone. On my way back to the station, I thought
about Rosemary Hix. Had she, somehow, taken violent

steps to get her fortune back? I thought about Frederick Collins, too. I couldn't imagine a man committing murder so as to be elected a town father, but it could be strange motive number 101. On the other hand, what was so strange about it? Look what other men had done for power.

Then, I realized I was well on my way toward assuming Hugo Hix was dead. Was that one of my come-from-nowhere hunches? Or was I bored already, hoping for some excitement, longing to prove to the people of Wellesley that they'd appointed themselves one hell of a police chief?

Sure, Hugo griped me plenty. But wish him dead? Better shape up, Knute, old turkey, you've got yourself a long, long turnpike to patrol.

❖❖❖❖❖❖❖

Three days later we had a freak thaw to go with our freak snowstorm. Overcoats got too heavy and dead-grass lawns were spongy. General conversation included the observation that winters weren't what they used to be; portents indicated that future New England winters would be (a) colder, a new ice age, or (b) hotter, thus melting the northern floes and inundating the coastlands.

Natick police called us. They'd come up with a body. Actually it was our body, they said, over the Wellesley line near the Stigmatine Fathers, a man's body floating in the Charles River, caught under the iron bridge on the road to the Stigmatine estate.

"Hugo?" I wondered aloud to Dennehy.

He shrugged. "Could be. Who else? Let's go and find out."

He drove, no sense in taking extra cars with the price of gas the way it is. Hayes and Stark went along in the back seat, they brought a camera. Dr. Jeffrey Talbot of the Board of Health was due to meet us there with the ambulance. He'd bring the canvas body bag. Chances were it was Hugo. As Dennehy said, who else could it be? Now we'd have something to go on. I heard myself thinking the things I was thinking and kicked myself mentally. The responsibility was getting to me, so soon. Would I feel the usual pity when looking on the dead? God, I hoped so. I didn't want to stop caring.

A couple of Natick officers were waiting for us along with a seminarian who'd taken a break from his studies at the Stigmatine Fathers only to spot a body curled around one of the bridge pilings near the shore. The seminarian looked sick, and the Natick men looked glad to see us.

Stark took some pictures from the bridge. The nude body lay face down, the legs moved feebly in the water. "That's not Hugo," said Dennehy.

"No. Too tall. Too thin." A whole new ball game. Yes, I felt sorry for whoever it was, and I felt, too, a peculiar kind of relief, which I didn't stop to analyze.

"We'll be getting along," one of the Natick cops announced. "Let us know if you need any help."

"He may belong to you, you know." I didn't blame them for running.

"But he's yours at the moment." The officer grinned, more of a grimace than a smile. His name was Boggs, he was young, fresh-faced, probably had high color when he wasn't facing a corpse.

"We'll get back to you," I promised, and they took off, cruiser wheels making the bridge rattle. Moments later our ambulance arrived and we all went down the banking.

"He hasn't been in the water long," Dr. Talbot observed as Hayes employed a hook to pull him closer.

"No? You can tell by looking?"

"Yes." We moved back a few steps so they could bring him up on the bank. Stark worked his camera. "It looks like . . ." The doctor bent, stared into the exposed face. Wearing gloves, Dennehy and Hayes began to slide the body into the canvas sack.

"It looks like what?"

We straightened up, the bag was closed.

"I'd rather wait until I get a better look, but I'd say he was dead when he was immersed. Dead for some time."

"What do you mean, some time?"

"Well, look at him. I'd say weeks, at least. Maybe longer."

I frowned. "You mean he may have been buried? Washed out of a grave?" I tried to think where the nearest cemetery was. The Charles flowed easterly to the sea, of course. There was a cemetery to the west, in South Natick.

"If so"—the doctor sounded puzzled—"it was a private grave."

"What do you mean?"

"I don't think he's been embalmed. It looks like the natural process of decomposition. I can't tell you anything for sure until we do a P.M., so don't ask me."

We watched in silence while the bag, on a stretcher, was put into the ambulance.

I sighed. "You've lived in Wellesley a long time, haven't you, Doc?"

"A little over thirty years."

"How many murders in those thirty years?"

"In this town?" He thought. "Maybe two—or three. They've been picking up lately. Like all over the world, times are changing."

"I was thinking maybe I was the Jonah. I've lived here five years and, if this is homicide, that will make the three coming in my time." I didn't add four—if Hugo fits the bill. I'd certainly expected this to be Hugo.

The doctor had a dry sense of humor. "Some people have all the luck." He headed for the ambulance.

"When can you let me know?"

"Tomorrow morning. I've got to get hold of the state pathologist . . ."

I urged, "As soon as you can." Stark photographed the bank and piling with a close-angle lens. Dennehy and Hayes poked around in the long brown grass, came up with nothing. I went to talk to the student priest.

"What's your name?"

"Brother Benedict."

"Your real name?"

"Michael Kelly."

"Home address?"

He gave me a street and number in South Boston.

"Tell me what happened. Why you came down here, when."

He looked almost like a thin girl with his young innocent face and his black robe. "The weather was so warm, I just thought I'd take a walk down to the river. I miss the water, you know, I grew up on the water, beside it. Anyway, I just slipped out a side door, I didn't want any company."

I nodded.

"Well, I almost didn't come because I started across the lawn and it's pretty boggy." He showed muddy shoes, even the hem of the robe was mud-marked. "But the road isn't so bad so I came that way"—he pointed—"which is why I ended up here at the bridge. You know, I wasn't looking for anything except maybe a fish. And I saw him. I didn't believe it at first. You know?" He blushed. "I didn't want him to be dead and I didn't want him to be there, but he was so I knew I had to do something about it. I ran back to the big house, found Father Martin and told him, privately. I didn't think it would be good if all the guys"—he blushed again—"the brothers came rushing down here. Father Martin called the Natick police and told me to come down and wait for them." He twisted his hands together. "That's all I know. I left the house about four o'clock and I found him. That's all I know."

"Oh, boy," murmured Dennehy at my elbow, "we'll have to question a houseful of padres."

Brother Benedict's eyes widened. "Oh, but you don't think . . . none of us was involved. That's just not possible."

"Get in the cruiser," I said. "We'll take you back."

"To Father Martin. Yes, you must speak to Father Martin. He will know how to explain."

The Stigmatine Fathers occupy what was once a large and elegant estate and they have kept it up quite well. The main house is large and well built. We found Father Martin in a library sitting room all paneled in oak. Father Martin was rotund, his face was smile-lined. Now he looked as grave as possible and asked, "Who was he? Do you know?"

"Not yet." The big room was empty except for Father Martin, Brother Benedict and the four of us, nor had I seen anyone in the chapel or hall. "Where is everyone?"

"At various duties. The kitchen crew is preparing dinner. Certain classes are being conducted. Others are meditating according to their schedules." He glanced fondly, I thought, at Brother Benedict. "This one was a temporarily lost sheep. He played hookey when he walked down to the river." The twinkle vanished. "The discovery was his penance."

"How many priests are here? Brothers? Are there any lay persons on the estate?"

"At present there are twenty priests and forty-nine brothers at Elm Bank. Although we are called the Stigmatine Fathers, our formal name is Elm Bank Seminary. Actually, we are located in Wellesley, but the perimeters of the estate touch on Dover and Natick. I telephoned the Natick force because I believed that bridge was on Natick land."

He was wandering. I got him back to the lay population to find that none lived on the estate at the moment. The seminarians did much of their own work.

"Is everyone accounted for?" I asked.

Father Martin nodded. "That's the first thing I did, took a roll call. All present and accounted for."

"How about in the past six months?" I had no idea how long the corpse had been a corpse, but six months sounded like a maximum figure.

"Six months?" Father Martin raised fuzzy blond brows, they matched the curly fringe that ringed the back of his head. "We've had no disappearances here, ever. Not in my time and my time surpasses five years."

"But men have come and gone in the past six months?"

"Yes."

"Can you trace them?"

"I believe so. I shall have to look into the files."

"Would you do that for me, please?"

"Yes, of course. I understand. You anticipate difficulty in identifying the victim."

"It's possible. He wore no clothing. If no one claims him, if the teeth and fingerprints give us no clues—it can be difficult." I had a hunch it would be. I felt it, as my mother likes to say, in my bones.

I told Father Martin that I might have to talk to the Elm Bank population, he said he would co-operate. He walked us to the entrance, giving me a thumbnail history of the place as we walked. "Did you notice the elms bordering the road? They are, naturally, the reason for the name Elm Bank. They were planted by Colonel John Jones, Jr., who built his mansion here on seventy-two acres bought in 1740. Later more land was acquired by the Cheneys and the Baltzells. The grounds are especially beautiful in season. You must come and visit us when we're abloom."

"Thanks. My wife would like to see the place."

"You are a Catholic, Chief Severson?"

"No, Father."

"Ah, well, no matter. I just thought your wife might like to join our ladies' organization. The ladies do wonderful things for Elm Bank. Nonetheless, we shall be most pleased to see you. All are welcome." He turned to the others. "Are you gentlemen of the faith?"

"I am," said Dennehy.

"Ah. Is Mrs.—Dennehy, wasn't it—active in our organization?"

"No, Father. She works."

"I shall have one of the ladies call on her. Employment does not interfere with many of our functions."

Out in the car, Dennehy said, "Whew. Anne will be trapped, you wait and see. There's nothing like a jolly father to get you working for the church."

"Will she mind?"

"Probably. We're not really practicing Catholics."

"My wife is always over at the Baptist Church," said Hayes from the back seat. "She sings in the choir."

"My wife's father is a Unitarian minister," I told them. "Up in Woodvale, New Hampshire."

"Unitarians are freethinkers, aren't they?" asked Stark. "I'm a Jehovah's Witness. That is, my wife is."

"That's the way it goes." Dennehy waxed philosophical. "Nearly every time it's the woman who tends to the religious aspect. Good thing, too, 'cause otherwise we'd all burn in hell."

"You know," Hayes spoke thoughtfully, "I think that John Doe was a sailor."

I jerked around to look at him. "A sailor? He looked too old to be a sailor. What makes you think that?"

"I just remembered—it didn't mean anything to me at the time, but I got to thinking about my wife being a Baptist and that got me thinking about before I was married, which took me back to the days when I was in the service, the Navy, and then I knew what it meant."

"What what meant?"

"I carried the feet, see, and on each foot was a little-bitty tattoo, you'd hardly notice it. One was a pig, I think, and the other a rooster. I didn't look close."

"A pig? A rooster?"

"Yeah. The old-time Navy guys used to do it. The idea was if you had a pig and a rooster you'd never drown because a pig gets so scared and swims so hard he cuts his throat with his sharp hoofs and a rooster gets so scared he has a heart attack, so either way you don't drown, see?"

Dennehy grunted. "Didn't do him much good. We fished him out of the water anyway."

"He didn't drown," Dr. Talbot told me. "He's been dead four or five months and he died from a fractured skull. He's a Caucasian male, aged about fifty-five. We can't check his teeth because he wore false teeth and they're missing. Fingerprints aren't going to help you too much because there isn't much left to test . . ."

"He was in the Navy, we think. If we could just get enough of a print to send to the Navy in Washington."

Dr. Talbot looked impressed. "I don't know how you got that."

"Tattoos on his feet. He had them, didn't he? A pig and a rooster?"

"Yes, that is, I guess a pig and a rooster, not too clear. What does that mean?"

I told him what Hayes had said.

"Is that so? Never heard it, but I was in the Army Medical Corps. Well, send your print man down, we'll do our best but I'm not promising too much . . ."

"A fractured skull. What kind of a weapon?"

"Can't tell. Anything from an auto accident to a poker. Too much time has passed, he's been buried too long . . ."

"Buried? Are you sure?"

"I think so. Dirt in the nostrils and ears that even the water didn't get out. But he had to be buried—or frozen. You just don't keep a corpse around without one or the other."

"Could be he was left on Elm Bank land somewhere, perhaps in a shallow grave, and the freeze followed by thaw caused the earth to heave and he either slid into the river or somebody put him in . . ." I was thinking fast. Not well, maybe, but fast.

"I can't tell you, conjecture is not my line. We medicos go on the evidence."

"Evidence," I laughed shortly. "That's a cop's middle name. Thanks, Doc, for—as they say in a business letter—your kind attention to this matter. I'll send Dennehy over with a fingerprint kit. He's less likely to turn green than the others."

"Not a pretty sight, even for me."

"Nor for me. What will we do with John Doe?"

"Bury him in the town lot unless you come up with an identification."

"How long can you wait?"

"A couple of days at the most."

"Okay. We'll get cracking."

"I think I'll skip lunch," Dennehy told me when he returned.

"Any luck?"

He shrugged. "Did what I could."

"Have one of the men run them into the Fargo building. Send a note marked RUSH in big letters. They can get action. Who do I know in there?" I couldn't come up with a name.

"There's a naval reserve captain here in town, a good guy. Maybe if you give him a call, he'll put some pressure on."

"If you know him, you call. I'll take over if he wants to speak to me." I had a message on my desk to phone Rosemary Hix, and I figured I'd better get at that.

"Aye, aye, sir." Dennehy gave me a mock salute and went out.

She answered on the first ring, sitting by the telephone? "Chief Severson, Mrs. Hix. Sorry I couldn't get back to you sooner."

"Was it Hugo?" Her voice was breathy with unshed tears—or excitement?

"I beg your pardon?"

"The body. I heard there was a body in the river. Was it Hugo?"

"No. No, it wasn't."

"Oh." A pause. "Who was it?"

"We don't know yet."

"You don't know? You mean, it could still be Hugo?" Animation came back into her voice.

"No, it couldn't be. He was older, there's no physical resemblance." I didn't want to go into ugly details.

"But, it could be? I mean, when you're in the water a long time, you can't really tell very well, can you?"

She was dead set on it being Hugo, it seemed. A natural reaction? She'd rather face the worst than wonder? Possible; nonetheless, she made my scalp crawl.

"We can tell." My voice was cold. "For one thing, he'd been dead for months, not days, and for another . . ."

"Oh." A definite letdown. "Then it couldn't have been Hugo."

I did not snarl, That's what I've been telling you! I said, gently, "No. It can't be."

Without another word, she hung up.

Brenda wanted to go Christmas shopping after dinner. I was definitely not in the mood, but we called Frances Porter in to sit with Lief and I drove her out to Natick Mall and Shopper's World, where we didn't find much of what we wanted. "I told you," I told her, "that you can find all the toys you want at Olken's right in Wellesley. As for your father and my mom and dad . . ."

"Yes, dear," said Brenda soothingly.

Before I went to bed, I called the station. Nothing yet from the Navy. Nothing new on Hugo. Nothing untoward anywhere. "It's a quiet night," said Thompson, the night sergeant.

With that thought in mind, I went to bed and, finally

(Who the devil was the John Doe? Where the hell was Hugo?) to sleep.

I was down in a deep dark well when the sound brought me up and out. "Knute!" whispered Brenda fearfully, "What is it?"

It was a long, drawn-out howling sound that at first I thought was animal, but the animal was forming words so I realized it was human. I couldn't make out the words right off but I did identify the accompanying sound as the breaking of glass.

Our bedside telephone rang. I picked it up, Mercy's voice said, "God, Knute, what's going on over at your place?"

The howling grew louder, more glass shattered. Lief began to cry, Brenda slid out of bed to go to him.

"I don't know," I told Mercy, "but if you'll hang up I'll try to find out."

She hung up.

I went to the window. There was a sliver of a new moon plus clouds and I couldn't see much other than a shadow in the driveway that looked like a car and another shadow, man-shaped, on our roofless front porch.

"Help!" screamed the shadow. "For God's sake, somebody help me! Help!" He was at the small-paned picture window beating on the glass, but the outer window was a solid sheet of glass, a storm window, double thickness, and he couldn't break it. Not yet.

I went to the phone, dialed the station. "Send somebody over here," I told Thompson. "There's trouble."

He sounded half asleep. "Who . . . ?"

"Christ, it's me. Severson." A shriek came from outside and a gigantic crash. "Get me a cruiser!" I shouted and dropped the phone.

I struggled into a robe. Brenda, holding Lief, was standing in the upper hall. "Stay here," I warned her and, slipperless, hurried down the stairs, almost tripping in the darkness.

In the foyer, I snapped on porch lights. I wanted to see him but I didn't want him to see me. The glass storm door that covered the front door was smashed, so I didn't open the inner door. A figure came to it in the light, I could see through the as yet unbroken glass side panels. He was dripping blood from both hands, his face was wild and he was screaming.

It was Rod Avery. I tried to speak to him, but he wasn't sane. I didn't dare open the wooden door, I wasn't sure I could handle him in his mental state and Brenda and Lief were upstairs—where the hell was the cruiser? The kid would bleed to death.

"Knute," Brenda hissed over the upper railing. I looked up. "Do you want your gun?"

"Not unless I have to. No, I don't want it. There's a cruiser coming." Where *was* it?

"Help! Somebody help me! I'm lost, lost! Help Me! Help me!" Agonizing cries in the black night; I'd heard the expression "a soul in hell," and this was it.

Lights came on the street, lights in houses. He was banging his head against the house and screaming. At last there were car lights coming up the hill, a screech of brakes, two men running up the walk.

I opened the front door and grabbed him. My reinforcements took him from the back. He struggled with almost superhuman strength. Now he was shouting something else, "He's dead. I'm going to die. He's dead. I'm going to die!"

Another car wheeled up. Thompson must have called them all in. When the two officers came up the steps, Avery suddenly collapsed in my arms. I could feel his blood soaking my robe.

"What the effing hell . . . ?" It was Davis who spoke, I recognized them now, Davis and Green, Hildreth and Stark.

"Get him to the hospital, on the double," I ordered. "I think he's on something. Either that or he's flipped. He's going to bleed to death. One of you guys go in, Brenda will give you some towels, use 'em for tourniquets, he's slashed himself breaking our windows. Brenda," I raised my voice to a shout, "towels!"

They took him off me and I followed Hildreth inside. "I'll follow you," I said, "I'll get some clothes on and follow you."

Brenda threw a pile of towels down the stairwell. They separated and Hildreth had to stop to pick them up. None of us was thinking very clearly.

"Knute," cried Brenda as I passed her. "Who is it?"

"The Avery boy. He's either as high as that moon or

he's off his rocker. Lock the door behind me when I go, I'll be back as soon as I can."

"But what does he want with us?" her eyes were wide with horror.

"Didn't you hear him?" I asked. "He wanted help."

❖❖❖❖❖❖❖❖

"It was LSD," I told a white-faced Laurie Avery. "He'll be okay, we think, but he had a very bad trip and they tell me there's no guarantee that it won't happen again even without another dose of the drug. Other than that, and some scars on his hands and arms from breaking glass, he's okay."

"Where did he get the LSD?" she spoke woodenly.

"In Boston. He told us where, I passed it along to the BPD. Could we sit down, Mrs. Avery? I have to ask some rough questions."

A self-deprecating smile came and went. "I'm not much of a mother, am I? I try my best, but . . ." She hugged herself, sat in a brocade chair, motioned me to the sofa.

"I haven't talked to him this morning yet, he's sleeping, but I talked to him—no, that's not right, I listened to him when he was on his trip. He heard about the body we took out of the Charles, he got it in his head that it was Hugo Hix. He was trying to tell me that he killed him, kept saying he was lost, but what was really bugging him, still is bugging him, I think, is that he thinks you killed Hugo."

Her eyes opened wide, very wide. "Me? Why would he think that I did anything to Hugo?" She put a trembling hand to her mouth.

"He thinks that you and Hugo were bedding down together." I'd made up my mind not to pussyfoot, I was in a plain-speaking mood. "He thinks you wanted Hugo to divorce his wife and marry you. He's got it in his mind that you're a woman who cares a great deal about appearances and reputations. Rod believes that you couldn't take a casual relationship for long. According to him, you live by the dictum 'What will my friends think?' So, he thinks, you lashed out—and the result was one dead Hugo deposited in the river."

She took her hand away from her mouth. "That's ridiculous. All of it. And it wasn't Hugo you found . . ."

"No, it wasn't." I seemed to spend a lot of time assuring people that the body in the river was not Hugo's. "But your son must have had some reason to believe you were sufficiently involved with Hugo Hix to have had a motive . . ." Despite my intent to say things right out, I found myself floundering in attempted niceties.

"Have you got a cigarette?" asked Laurie Avery.

"Sorry. I don't smoke."

She got up, then made her way across the room to an ornate breakfront, which, when opened, turned out to be a bar. She found cigarettes in a carton, tore off cellophane, rummaged around for a lighter. When she'd lit her cigarette she said, without looking at me, "I don't suppose you drink, either."

"Not now. Sometimes, but not now."

"In the middle of the morning, you mean. Well, neither do I, but you've just given me reason to start." She pulled a decanter toward her, splashed Bourbon or rye, couldn't tell, into an etched glass. She drank it down, a straight out-of-the-west down-the-gullet drink.

She turned around to face me, empty glass in her hand. "I spend my days trying to be all things to all people. A foolish endeavor, all things considered." She dimpled, and it was a not quite rational smile. "That's a pun, isn't it?" She sobered. "Nothing to laugh about. It's my upbringing, you see. Laurie, the lady. But Laurie is a woman and a woman needs a man. A lady needs a husband—the first one was no joy. But a man—these days the young people play house without a qualm. I can't. I have to find someone with something to give, also with something to lose because he must be discreet. Must be!" Her color was high now, she turned abruptly, refilled the glass.

When she'd tossed that off, she began again. "Do you think Hugo was my choice? Yech. He was the Lest I could do. You, a handsome man like you, if I made advances, even hinted, you'd run, wouldn't you? Wouldn't want to get mixed up with a mixed-up female. That's the way it is with all the desirable ones. So it's the Hugos of this world who fit the somewhat altered bill. Bargain rates for bed and board! I come cheap!" She laughed.

Quietly I asked, "Is Rod right? Did you kill him?"

She threw the glass into the fireplace. She had a good arm, the fireplace was all the way across the room. "I wouldn't bother. He meant nothing, one way or another. He was convenient, just barely. I haven't seen him for two weeks at least, maybe three. If you want to know the truth, Hugo Hix made me sick. I make me sick!" She turned away from me.

I stood. "You're well off, Mrs. Avery. Maybe you have less problems because of that, maybe more. I've got a suggestion if you'll take it. Your son needs you, badly. He needs to believe in you. Maybe he did once, I don't know. I'd guess it was all right once, else he wouldn't take it so hard. Anyway, I suggest you take him someplace, someplace warm and pleasant and quiet where you can concentrate on him. Could be it's not too late, could be it is. If he were my son and I had the means, I'd try my damndest to save him. And if you can't help him, then you'll know and be able to find somebody else. Believe me, he needs help."

She didn't say anything and I had nothing else to say. I left quietly.

The Navy captain (reserve) reported back that there was no soap so far on the fingerprints of John Doe. "There wasn't much to go on," Dennehy reminded me. "Part of a thumbprint and two fingers of the left hand."

"We better bury him," said Dr. Talbot.

We did.

No news either on Hugo Hix.

What the hell, Christmas was coming and most people put unpleasant thoughts out of their minds. Except maybe for Rosemary Hix. Laurie and Rod Avery were in Palm Beach, I heard. As for me, holding unpleasant thoughts was part of my job. And, just in case I forgot that, I had daily phone calls from either Kendall Owens, Alfreda Burke, Sowerby and/or any combination of the three. Where was Hugo Hix? Tones changed, it seemed, from friendly polite to not so friendly to not so polite.

That question caused me some sleepless nights. I wondered if I'd made the right move in accepting the chief's job. Then, in the mornings, I told myself, we'll find him. If not today, tomorrow. We'll find him.

But the days went by and there was no sign of Hugo.

❖❖❖❖❖❖❖

Doddy, shopping list in hand, set out to collect Christmas gifts. Mother's present, unfortunately, had to be paid for—it was a new permanent wave at the neighborhood beauty salon. But for the Terences and for Clarice and maybe even a little something for Chief Severson's little boy (That would be a nice gesture, wouldn't it?) there were the throng-filled stores glittering with Christmas goodies. She'd picked out a necklace of baroque pearls at Filene's for Clarice. Clarice liked gaudy jewelry, and the pearls were hanging so conveniently at the far corner of the counter where the salesgirls seldom seemed to come.

The Terence gift was always a problem. She longed to buy something very special for Andy, but of course she couldn't so she always looked for something nice for the house. It had to be small enough to fit in her shopping bag but it had to be just right and that took some looking around. She'd finally decided on an exquisite crystal and gold paperweight at Marco Polo's. It was in a glass open-faced case at the front of the store, a locale always filled with people at this time of the year. So that left only the little Severson child, well, that should be simple enough—some sort of toy at Olken's.

She had trouble finding a parking space, and when she did it was over at the Tailby lot so she decided to stop in at Olken's first. A nice toy, nothing too grand . . . she enjoyed shopping around the toy department, becoming a bit sad that she had neither children nor nieces and nephews. She hummed "Away in a Manger" as she walked up the street, thinking how lucky she was, Hugo had vanished and just before he was about to tell Chief Severson that he'd seen her tucking a box of chocolates in her shopping bag at the Wellesley Pharmacy. Somebody up there certainly liked Doddy Miller, she reflected.

No matter, this would be her last sortie. After tonight she would take a solemn vow—never, never again.

Never. Another dreadful word like patience and duty.

❖❖❖❖❖❖❖

We got very busy the week before Christmas. You'd think that all that peace and love floating around in December would slow things down, but *"au contraire"* as my buddy Benedict says. Ask any cop, there are more shopliftings, assaults, burglaries, suicides and traffic accidents then than at any other time of the year. On top of everything else we had a good blizzard on the twentieth, over twelve inches of snow and a freeze set in right after so the streets were icy and the snow lay in crusty mounds.

Still pending were the disappearance of Hugo Hix, the identity of the Charles River John Doe (I'd urged the Navy to keep trying, they were good enough to take care of the burial in the plot reserved for ex-servicemen) and the department budget, the latter being the reason I was in my office the night of December 23 at 10 P.M. struggling to get the damned thing finished and in Sowerby's hands before Christmas.

When my phone rang I swore and thought, Now what? I picked it up, took a deep breath and said, "Chief Severson speaking."

"I told you," cried a feminine voice I didn't recognize right off. "You can't say I didn't tell you and what did you do about it? Slap a wrist or two, that's all. I'm going to write a letter to the townsman!"

"Who is this?" I asked brusquely. "What's your problem?"

"This is Mrs. Clifford Roberts, that's who! And that woman, that crazy woman, she needs psychiatric care, I tell you!"

"Miss Draggon? What has she done now?"

"Right out in front of anyone who passes by. The children saw it, they're delighted with the snow, of course, and a snowman just thrills them. Well, when they told me, I went right over there to make sure and they weren't making things up, I assure you. I saw it with my own eyes!"

"Saw what, Mrs. Roberts?" I was trying my best to be patient but the odds were against me.

"The pornographic snowman! Haven't you been listening to what I've been saying?" Her voice was on that high track again, she screeched in my ear.

"A pornographic snowman? You mean . . . ?"

"I mean all the parts are there, and exaggerated, too! I'm a broad-minded person, all my friends will tell you that, but I've never been so shocked in my life. To think I'd see such a thing in Wellesley. . . . I want you to know, Chief Severson, that I consider you totally inept. Last time you ignored me, I took my complaint to the Board of Selectmen but all I got from him was lip service. At least that was something, though. I don't even get lip service from you!"

"I'll drive out there right away, Mrs. Roberts. I assure you I'll take care of it. I'll handle it personally." This one obviously required a hoop jumper. All right, I'd jump, wearing frills and clown cap. I couldn't believe that Florence Draggon had snow-sculptured a pornographic snowman, maybe some smart-ass kid in the neighborhood was the culprit.

I got rid of Mrs. Roberts, stretched and stared bleary-eyed at the budget. One clear-eyed double check in the morning and I'd hand it to Sowerby. Ten thirty-five. Okay, I'd drive out to Schaller Lane, then home to bed. Tomorrow would be a long day, we'd have to put that tricycle together tomorrow night after Lief had gone to sleep. Nothing, it seemed, came assembled anymore.

It was cold out, damned cold, the stars looked fresh-cut. It took a few minutes for the car to warm up, so I sat and let the motor idle until all systems sounded go.

There wasn't much traffic on Route 16, only a couple of cars near St. Andrew's Church, one van turning into the college at the golf course. I drove carefully past the Hunnewell estates, the road was on the slick side and curvy. Christmas lights sparkled on a couple of houses up ahead in South Natick. I turned off on Schaller Street, lights on inside the Roberts house, a tree blinked on and off behind a picture window. I turned again, into Schaller Lane. My wheels skidded slightly, the road surface felt like virgin territory. Not much traffic on this cul-de-sac.

The Draggon house had candles with white bulbs at all its long, narrow windows. In the arch-topped window above the front-porch roof was a trio of the same candles. Traditional and attractive, I thought. Certainly not in keeping with—my car lights lit up the snowman and I said, involuntarily, "My God! She wasn't kidding."

The unbelievable physique of the snowman had been carefully modeled. So, if kids had done it, why hadn't Miss Draggon gone out and erased the offense with a shovel blow? Ten minutes of eleven, if I waited until morning I'd get hell from Mrs. Roberts and I wasn't sure I'd blame her. Broad-minded, sure, but . . . I switched off my car lights, got out and crunched my way up to the porch.

Florence Draggon, wearing some kind of fancy, padded dressing gown opened the door. "Why, it's Chief Severson! What in the world are you doing out this way so late?" She looked over my shoulder at my hastily parked car. "Run out of gas? Come in, come in. Gracious, it's cold for this time of year. Let me take your coat, sit down and get warm. Would you like some mulled cider?"

She was chattering inanely—she hadn't sounded this way the last time. Her eyes, concentrating on mine, shone with excitement. Subtract thirty-five or so years and she was a very young girl greeting her lover. My back felt chilled, so I didn't even unbutton my coat.

"Miss Draggon, that snowman out there. Who's responsible for that?"

Her eyes grew even brighter, her face crinkled and she put a stubby hand over her mouth to suppress her giggles. "Veronica," she said between her fingers. "Veronica did it."

"Where is she?"

She sobered and became haughty. "In bed, of course. It's late. Much too late for strangers to come calling."

"I'd like to speak to Mrs. Digby, please. Would you ask her to come down?"

"Why? Why do you want to speak to her? Because of Mr. Snowman? There's no law against making a snowman." She began again to laugh and the hand moved back to her mouth to hide it.

"No, there's no law. I'd just like to speak to her. She can't be asleep. There are lights upstairs. Would you ask her to come down?"

The unexpressionless face returned. There'd been an actor when I was a kid, Edgar Kennedy, who'd had a trick of laughing, then passing his hand over his face, literally wiping the laughter away. Florence Draggon's changes of expression came and went like that. It was spooky.

"I'll see if she's up there," she told me.

"What do you mean—you said she was."

"She was. But she might be downstairs now. We have a back staircase, you know. Veronica may have come down while we were talking. She hates to miss anything."

I felt like shaking the old girl. I wondered if there was someone in the family who could keep them in line. It seemed to me that they were losing their stuffing.

"I'll go upstairs and see," said Miss Draggon abruptly. Maybe she'd been reading my mind.

I moved farther into the sitting room, where a fire was blazing in the fireplace. I heard her footsteps going up, then nothing. I studied the photograph collection on the mantel, a framed picture showed a pair of girls looking much alike and wearing identical clothes characteristic of the thirties, or at least what I assumed they wore in the thirties. And there was a rather faded studio-type photo of a man and woman formally dressed in clothes from an even earlier era. The man had a stern, heavy face and big, stocky body, and the woman vaguely resembled the sisters. Mama and Papa, no doubt. A wedding picture beside that showed a young white-gowned Veronica clinging to the arm of a tall thin man in a morning coat. Veronica looked triumphant. The thin man, Mr. Digby I presumed, wore a self-conscious smile and showed a mouthful of teeth accented by a gap between the two middle ones. Except for that he looked like a thousand guys I'd seen before. Veronica looked like Veronica twenty-five years before. I peered at the picture of the two of them, Veronica was the one with the expectant expression, Florence looked glum.

Where was she, anyway? I stepped out into the hall and looked up the stairway. As I stood, looking up, wondering whether to call out, a door opened and shut and a figure came into view. As she passed beneath the light on the upper landing, I saw it was Mrs. Digby. "I'm sorry," she trilled, coming down the steps, "I had to make myself presentable." She smirked and added coyly, "I was in bed."

"I'm sorry to disturb you," I said coolly. Something about Veronica Digby put me off. Not that Florence Draggon put me at my ease, but at least she came across as real. In my opinion, Veronica Digby was a phoney.

"Come into the sitting room," she invited. "We'll sit down and chat."

She had gotten herself all togged out. Not a dark hair out of place, full make-up and a red and gold fussy robe. "Florence will be up in a minute," she told me. "She went down to the cellar to bring up some cider, we'll have refreshments." Another smirk. Lipstick on her teeth again. Ugh.

"I didn't hear her come down."

"She went by the back stairs. Sit here, Chief Severson." She patted the cushions on the unoccupied side of the carved sofa. "The fire feels delightful. I always love a fire in the fireplace, don't you?"

God, I thought, is she making a play for me? I sat, but as far from her as the length of the sofa allowed.

"Aren't you going to take your coat off?" Was she wearing false eyelashes? I thought so.

"No, thanks. I won't be long. It's about that snowman out on your lawn . . ."

She ignored that. "Papa always said that wearing a coat in the house brought on influenza. Papa lived to be ninety-two."

Anything—almost—to make her happy. I unbuttoned my overcoat and slid out of it. "Mrs. Digby," I said while shucking the coat, "you don't seem the type of woman who would do something in bad taste . . ."

She giggled. I frowned, apparently she thought it was funny. I went on, "I don't know if there's a law against it, but surely we don't need to go to legal lengths to settle . . ." She'd giggled again.

"Of course," she said, "Papa died of influenza, so I don't know that Papa's advice was all that good."

I decided that the lady needed psychiatric help. Maybe what I should do was get out of there, dismantle—no, I guess dismember was the word—the snowman and send somebody from the Human Relations Service over tomorrow—ah, tomorrow was Christmas Eve, it could wait until after Christmas, couldn't it? She wasn't dangerous, just off center. Senility—at her age? Could be, it all depended on the blood vessels, as I understood it. And heredity?

"Where is Florence?" she asked. "We must offer some hospitality." She leaned forward confidentially. "If you have the impression that Florence is lacking the social graces, it's because she spent so many years caring for

Papa and for Mama. She didn't get out among people very often."

Okay, I'd come at it from her angle. "You left when you got married?"

"Oh, before that. Papa would never have permitted me to marry George Digby, he wasn't even an officer. He would have considered him beneath me. Papa was very strict. I ran away from home." The smirk seemed pitiful this time. "It was very brave of me."

Aha, maybe that explained something. Young Veronica had gotten away; old Veronica, a widow, returned to the trap. Who was it who said it's easier to live in a madhouse than to spend the day there? Florence seemed more at ease because she was used to living in seclusion at the end of Schaller Lane. What had her life been like? Lousy, I could bet. "How old were you when you ran away?"

She looked proud. "I left on my thirtieth birthday. I was very clever about it. I'd been taking money from the household account for years—Papa wouldn't let us work, of course, and he didn't believe in allowances. I didn't take any clothes or anything, he would have noticed. I just walked out of the house in the clothes I was wearing. I told them I was going to Cooper's Drug Store in South Natick Center. That's an easy walk, you know. There I caught the bus to Natick and Framingham and at Framingham I bought a train ticket to New York City. Papa would never find me in New York City." She jerked her head, her voice sharpened. "Did you hear that?"

"What?" I hadn't heard anything, didn't hear anything now.

"Excuse me a moment, I thought I heard Florence . . ." She hurried out of the room while I listened hard. I heard her footsteps for a few moments only, then all was silence. I looked at my watch, nearly midnight. I'd have given most anything to go, I was beat. I decided when they came back I'd make my good-byes and take care of the snowman personally.

"Chief Severson!" I heard her call from the hallway, there was panic in her tone.

"Yes? What is it, Mrs. Digby?"

Her eyes were wide, frightened. "Please come! The bulb has burned out in the cellar and Florence has fallen. I'm afraid she's badly hurt!"

I went with her. She held a big flashlight in her hand, two feet long at least, which lit the cellarway, showing the steep wooden steps when she aimed it for me from behind. There was a sharp angle, steps turned left, walls of great huge boulders, whitewashed but cobwebbed. The air was damp but surprisingly warm. It had the feel of a tunnel down there, of course, shaped like the house, long and narrow. "Where is she?" I panted.

The flashlight indicated a door ahead. "In there. Oh, do hurry!"

I pushed open the door, heard it bang against stone. Metal against stone? A metal door? I heard a woman cry out too. That was the last thing I thought because something crashed down in the darkness, something that brought the darkness to me and I passed into nothingness with no time for pain or regret.

❖❖❖❖❖❖❖❖

I was about to wake up and I didn't want to wake up. I hadn't had enough sleep, for one thing. God, I was tired, and I had a headache. A bad headache, the great king headache of headaches. Why did I have a headache, had I tied one on last night?

Last night.

I opened my eyes and moved them, not my head, from side to side.

I was lying on some kind of cot covered by a thin mattress on a metal frame. I was covered with a quilt.

I was in an enclosed area—no, not totally enclosed. The bottom walls were of wood, old-fashioned tongue-and-groove panels once varnished brown. Three of the top walls were covered with ten-inch boards placed horizontally; one wall, the one I faced, was open at the top and I could see out—that is, if I raised my head. Since that took some doing, I decided to lay it down again—on a pillow?

—yes, a pillow, and wait until later. The wall with the opening was a door. There was a latch on the lower partition. The open portion was maybe three feet deep. A—a stall? For a horse? Or a cow? A wooden box on the right wall could have been for grain, a water bucket hung on a hook above that. I looked up at the ceiling. Crossbeams under flooring. Pipes running along that. I was in a stall in Miss Draggon's cellar. Miss Draggon—what happened to Miss Draggon? What happened to me?

"Hey!" I tried my voice, shaky. "Anybody there?" I put my hand up, found a bandage on the back of my head. That's where the pain came from.

"Are you all right?" asked a woman's voice. Miss Draggon's voice? Not quite, unless her injury had distorted it as it had mine. Mrs. Digby's voice?

"Who's there?" I asked.

"Veronica Digby. Who are you?"

I groaned. She had flipped, I was afraid of that. All the signs were there. "Chief of Police Severson. What happened? What happened to me?"

"She hit you with the flashlight. I was afraid—it's a very large flashlight and she's very strong. She doesn't look it, but she is."

I pushed myself up on my elbows. To hell with my headache. "Who hit me with the flashlight?"

"My sister, of course."

"But you said . . ."

"I tried to warn you, but it was too late."

I started to swing my legs off the side of the cot, intending to sit upright. There was a clanking sound, something dragged one ankle. Good God, there was a metal cuff around my right ankle, a chain ran from the cuff to the back of the cot, out of sight behind. I pulled at it, it was longer than I thought. Could I get to the door? "What is this chain on my ankle? What's going on here?"

Her answer was a deep sigh.

"Come closer so I can see you," I insisted. "I want to see who I'm talking to."

"I can't. I'm chained, too, and I can't get out, either. Can you come to the door? We can see each other then, if you can come to the door."

I set my feet solidly on the floor and got myself up. It was maybe six feet to the stall door, it looked as wide as an eight-lane highway. I used the wall to keep myself upright and to propel myself forward. The ankle chain stopped me a foot or so from the opening. Directly across from me was the twin of my stall, looking out at me was a woman I had never seen before.

Oh, she looked something like Florence, all right. And she somewhat resembled the Veronica in the wedding picture upstairs. But her blue eyes were sunken and her face was lined and her hair was not dark but a dirty white.

"You're not—you're Veronica?" I stammered.

She tried to smile. Her mouth trembled. "I'm not sure anymore. When I came here I was Veronica, Mrs. George Digby, née Draggon. That was—six months ago, I think. More or less. What day is it?"

"It is—it should be—Christmas Eve. December twenty-fourth."

"We arrived on June thirteenth. An unlucky day."

"We?"

"George and I. He retired June first. We were going on a long trip, around the world, we hoped. We thought we should visit Florence first." She laughed, there were tears in her laughter. "I thought we should visit Florence first. George wasn't keen on it."

I felt the bandaged lump on my head. As sore as a boil! "I don't understand—my head isn't working too well. You weren't the one who brought me down here last night. Who was that?"

"Don't you know?" We heard the sound of a door opening and steps descending at the same time. "Here she comes," she whispered.

"Good morning, good morning!" Florence Draggon came into view, blue eyes sparkling, white hair fluffed around her head. "I've brought breakfast. Did you sleep well?"

"What the hell is going on here?" I demanded. It was a very good question, even though I didn't sound as authoritative as I intended—my head hurt too much when I yelled. What was going on? I didn't believe it. I'd fallen and hit my head and I was hallucinating.

"I hope you like scrambled eggs, Chief Severson. It's easier when I serve down here. I do believe they stay hot longer. Here you are." And she rested a full tray on the top of the door. I could reach it, but I couldn't reach her, not even her hands. They were safe on the far side of the tray.

"Take it," she urged, beaming, the eager hostess. I grabbed at the tray, as the dishes rattled. There was no place to set it except the cot. The chain scraped the cement floor as I moved across it.

Stay cool, Knute, I cautioned myself. She was across the way, serving Veronica. Veronica. If that was Veronica, then who . . . ? "Miss Draggon," I spoke quietly, "will you kindly explain why I am in this cubicle with a gash in my head and a shackle on my ankle?"

She twirled to twinkle at me. "I struck you with my flashlight. Actually it isn't my flashlight, it's Papa's flashlight. And you are restrained because that's what happens when you're naughty. Many's the time Veronica and I were chained here when Papa was alive, weren't we, Veronica?"

"Yes," Veronica sounded resigned, "many's the time."

Mrs. Clinton Roberts was right as rain—the lady was batty. All right, play along with her. "What have I done that's—naughty?"

She eyed me archly. "I'm sure you'll realize if you just put your mind to it. Papa always said that dirty minds needed to be cleansed. Such a comment on Veronica's ice sculpture! I went out and destroyed it early this morning."

I shut my eyes to get things in focus, opened them to ask, "How could Veronica have made the snowman when she's down here?"

"I don't mean that Veronica," said Florence sweetly. "I mean my Veronica. You see, each of us has a Florence side and a Veronica side."

"So . . ." I spoke slowly, "when you put on a black wig and make-up and different clothes, that's your Veronica."

She was obviously delighted with my cleverness. "Of course. You're the only one to guess. Not even that Veronica's friends could tell the difference. But then, they hadn't seen her in years and years." She regarded her sister. "She's aged terribly, don't you think?"

"Miss Draggon, I sincerely apologize for any risqué thoughts I might have had about the snowman. I do beg your pardon." I felt like an idiot, but I wanted out.

"A handsome apology, wouldn't you say, Sister dear? Eat your breakfast before it gets cold. I'm going up for mine. It's a beautiful day out, cold and sunny . . ."

"Miss Draggon"—I'd had quite enough—"unlock this shackle and let me out of here. I'm a busy man, I'm needed at the station and my wife will be frantic wondering where I am."

"In due time, sir. In due time. If you do as you're told, your penance will be over all the faster." She turned and vanished from my view.

"Wait a minute," I yelled, "you're committing a crime, don't you know that? My officers will come looking for me, they'll see my car!"

Her footsteps ceased, began again, returning. She stood once more at the door, not close to it, a couple of feet back where I couldn't possibly reach. "But your car isn't in the driveway anymore."

"Where the . . . where is it?"

"In the barn. Next to Papa's automobile. It's quite a large barn with solid doors. No one will ever know it's there."

"How did it get there? I thought you couldn't drive."

"I can't drive." She gave me one of her beaming smiles. "But my Veronica can." She turned away once more, her last words came as she retreated. "Veronica found a very nice gun in your glove compartment. I'm afraid of guns, but they fascinate Veronica."

"Jesus Christ," I whispered reverently.

I ate what I could. I felt lousy. I had another problem, too. "Mrs. Digby," I asked, "what do we do about bath-room facilities?"

"You see that bucket on the wall? Use that. She will bring water and soap when she returns, you'll at least be able to wash. Oh, what I wouldn't give for a hot bath!"

All the comforts of home. But she'd have to open the door sooner or later, wouldn't she? And when she did, ankle chain or no ankle chain, Florence Draggon and I were going around and around. In the meantime, I needed to lie down, to close my eyes; my head was killing me. I needed to think. If I closed my eyes, maybe when I opened them this would be a bad trip or a dream. It couldn't really be happening, a little old lady named Florence Draggon couldn't have her sister and the chief of police locked up in her cellar. Fantastic. Unreal. Impossible.

When I opened my eyes, I heard voices. Low voices arguing. ". . . and I've given up hope for myself but you have no cause to continue this way. What will happen to you, Florence? Can't you see what will happen to you?"

"Of course I can see. I am not without wits. That *is* my cause, I have no alternative. What does it matter now? In for a penny, in for a pound, as Papa used to say. This is my home, I have plenty of money, I'm quite comfortable here. Why should I let anyone take me out of it? And they would, you know, they indeed would."

"Dear God." Veronica was close to tears. "I should never have left without you. I should have taken you with me!"

"But I wouldn't have gone. Leave Papa and Mama? That would have been wicked. It was bad enough for you to go, but if I had left them alone . . . how would they have managed? I would never, never have forgiven myself."

"And you've never forgiven me."

"Oh, I forgave you long ago. Mama, too. But Papa hasn't. That's why you're being punished, don't you see? Perhaps one day he'll tell me that's enough, but until then, well, I have no other choice, have I?"

"Florence, Papa has been dead for years."

"I know that! Honestly, Veronica, sometimes you act as though I'm mindless. But I know how he feels, we always had that special relationship, each could tell what the other was thinking without speaking. After you left, it became even more so. Do you know, when he was displeased, he wouldn't have to say a word or move a finger? I'd come down here and shut myself in and I'd stay until he'd forgiven me. What would you call that, mental telepathy?"

"I know what I'd call it," Veronica's voice was low.

And I knew what I'd call it, too. I'd blundered into a madhouse, that was the plain and obvious truth. Here was Knute Severson, chief of Wellesley police, caged like a wandering jackass by a neurotic little old lady considered eccentric but harmless. Harmless, hah! But no matter, when the time came that a little-old-lady-in-tennis-shoes type could keep a mature, healthy male imprisoned in her cellar, I'd give it all up. I'd simply bide my time, find my opportunity, grab her in a half nelson or reasonable facsimile and convince her to let me go. And I'd better do it at the first opportunity, because I didn't want to egg her into waving my .38 around. No doubt, she knew nothing about guns, but her ignorance made her potentially dangerous. I didn't need Miss Draggon with a gun in hand—she was bad enough wielding a flashlight. My head still pained and I felt drowsy. I probably had a slight concussion. I'd lie down, leaving the breakfast tray and the bucket on the floor but well inside the door. When she came to collect them, I'd collect her, that was my plan.

I fell asleep.

Sound asleep.

The strong, experienced, mature cop closed his jaded eyes and slept like a baby. When I awoke, the tray was gone, the clean bucket back in place.

My watch told me it was four thirty-four. I silently called myself several uncomplimentary names before I sat up. My headache was almost gone. I felt much better. Okay, jerk, now put an end to this nonsense. When she came again with a dinner tray?

I got up and walked to the end of my chain. By staying to the right, I could reach farther than I could from center or left. Veronica Digby was lying on her cot, and she appeared to be napping. Okay, I'd use the time to check out the chain. Where was its weakest link? To what was it attached? I followed the links back to the wall behind my bed, feeling in my right-hand pocket as I went a small, pearl-handled gadget that came from Switzerland, which Brenda had given me. I used it for fingernail cleaning, it had a file and tiny scissors. Yes, I had it, I could possibly manage to unscrew or pry out the plate of the chain, it had to be attached to something. . . . The chain disappeared into the stone wall. Right through a circular aperture—a drill hole it appeared to be—went the links of the chain. I bent down and put an eye to the hole. I could barely glimpse a different kind of light at the far end, daylight—that is to say at this time of day in New England in December, twilight. The chain ran right through the stone foundation to the outside. Cold air came through the hole, very cold air. There was no way I could reach the end of the chain.

I backed off, sat on the bed and looked at the chain it-self. Heavy links, a good grade of quarter-inch steel, each link about an inch in circumference. I began to test each one. If there was a weak one, I couldn't find it. So much for old mottoes.

"Are you awake?" asked Veronica. "I told Florence to let you sleep. I thought you needed rest more than lunch, although I must say the grilled-cheese dreams were deli-cious. Florence puts tomato slices on top of the cheese and bread and grills them in the oven . . ."

"What time is dinner served?" I was back in the nuthouse, where concern was expressed for food and rest but all the time I was locked in a stall and chained to a wall.

"Papa always dined promptly at six-thirty. Florence never deviated from that dinner hour."

Six-thirty. An hour and a half, more or less, to wait . . . Brenda would be upset, but if I didn't make it home on Christmas Eve, she'd be frantic . . . and mad as a wet hen . . . what kind of scurrying activity currently occu-pied Wellesley's police force? What kind of trail had I left? Couldn't have done better if I'd planned the Great Getaway . . . at the station, the only person who saw me leave was the night deskman. I'd said not word one about my conversation with Mrs. Roberts. Was it possible that she'd spouted off to Jenks at the desk before he turned her over to me? Possible. But not probable. If Jenks knew who'd called, then why hadn't they checked out Mrs. Roberts, who would tell them about the pornographic

snowman whereupon they'd come here? How did I know
they hadn't? Now as I listened, I realized I couldn't hear
anything down here. No window in my—okay, Knute, go
on and call it a cell—in my cell. An electric light bulb
shone from a porcelain fixture in the ceiling corner. Even
if I yelled my lungs out, who's to hear? Or see? I could
imagine an officer—say, Dennehy—ringing Miss Draggon's
doorbell. Excuse me, ma'am, have you seen Chief Severson? Have I seen who? Chief Severson, Wellesley police.
We understand that he came to see you about a snowman. . . . About a what? A snowman. But there isn't any
snowman. According to our informant, there was a snowman she considered offensive. . . . Really, young man, do
you feel all right? Come in and get warm, would you like
some cider and gingerbread? I haven't seen your Chief
Severson, have you lost him? Oh yes, it would go on like
that until even Dennehy, one of my brightest, would go
away, head reeling.

My car, Miss Draggon had said, was in the barn. If
Dennehy would only ask to look around—car tracks, my
tracks in the drive, would they show up? The snow had
been maybe a foot deep. I'd made ruts, Dennehy would
have driven over them (if he came), he'd realize someone
had driven in, but what would that mean to him? A relative, friend, salesman, delivery man had visited? Why
should his suspicion mechanism be triggered? Nobody
would believe—I mean nobody—that that cuddly-type little old lady with the shining blue eyes had chained "pets"
in her cellar.

All right, so I had to get myself out.

All right, so I would.

I looked at my watch. All that heavy thought had taken ten minutes.

"Are you a married man, Mr. Severson?" asked Veronica from across the way.

"Yes, I am. And a father—my wife will be very concerned by now. Christmas Eve and all that." I tried to sound slightly pitiful.

"Of course she will!" Veronica was all sympathy. "George and I weren't blessed with children. What kind do you have? Boys or girls?"

"One boy, Lief. He's five, all excited about Santa Claus. Let's don't talk about him, the thought upsets me. How long have you been down here, Mrs. Digby?"

"Let's see, we came home in June . . . George had retired and it costs so much to live in New York, especially on a small pension and social security, so I said to George, why not go to Wellesley and live with Florence, she'll welcome the company and our share of expenses will be so much less . . . then we'll be able to make that trip . . ."

"You don't mean you've been down here since June?" I was appalled.

"No, no, I was merely putting events in chronological order. As I was saying, George and I came here in June, and then George died, June twenty-second to be exact, and we buried him the next day so I've been down here since June twenty-third."

I got up and went toward the door to look on her. "That's six months. Your sister has kept you locked up for six months. I'd be climbing the walls if I were you, but you seem very calm in this intolerable situation."

Veronica came as close as she could and smiled out at me. "You sound so concerned. Isn't that sweet of you? I suppose many people couldn't accept the situation, but if they'd been brought up by our father, they'd know the real meaning of forbearance."

Papa must have been something. Papa was maybe the clue to getting out of here. "Who was your father?" I asked. "What did he do for a living?"

"Papa farmed when we were young. We owned quite a bit of land, in fact we still do, although not as much as then. Friends talked him into selling off what is now Schaller Street—there was some South Natick acreage as well. He raised cattle and grew their feed. Mama had a wonderful vegetable garden, I can still taste the fresh asparagus from the asparagus patch. But then, well, Papa used to say 'the enemy is approaching'; what he meant was that houses were being built and houses meant people, people who wandered over our property at will. Vegetables began to disappear from Mama's garden, the cattle would wander out onto the new roads and one was killed by an automobile. Papa said it was the end of an era. He sold the cattle, Mama stopped growing vegetables and that was when Papa began to change."

"Change? How?"

"He never was overly friendly, but after a while he

wouldn't see anybody but us. He wouldn't go out in his car anymore, so I had to drive Mama to the market—either that, or we'd have groceries delivered. Papa became very bitter, he said God might as well call off the noble experiment because man was a beast and there was no way of teaching a beast to be a man. Not that Papa was religious, because he wasn't. He said religion was all a trick and a sham. He didn't believe in a lot of things—telephones or radios or all that. Mama had to insist—and Mama seldom insisted—that Florence and I be allowed to finish high school. He didn't think much of modern education either."

No wonder the sisters were weird. And Florence more than Veronica because, "at least you got out."

"It wasn't easy. I'll never forget the one time I brought George home. We'd been married a couple of years, I'd been writing to Florence and she'd written back that she felt Papa was grieving because I'd left so I thought if George and I paid them a visit, Papa would see that George was good and kind and everything was all right. Well! Was I ever wrong, Papa acted just terrible. I hate to say it but I was really afraid of him. So we didn't even stay one night. We left and never saw Papa again."

"It must have been tough for Florence and your mother."

"I thought so, but they didn't. They didn't mind Papa's ways as much as I did. Florence was Papa's girl from the time we were little. And to Mama, Papa was God. The only time I ever remember her going against him was about our going to school." She smiled at me. "It wasn't so strange, really. That's the way things used to be. The father was the head of the house. Weren't your parents like that?"

I thought of my mother and father living happily in Florida, making new friends almost daily. "No. Not like that."

"That's because you're young. A generation before, that's the way it used to be."

I didn't bother to argue that contention. "Your sister is ill, you realize that? She needs psychiatric help."

She cocked her head. "Florence has her eccentricities, that's true. But if you'd lived the life she's lived, you'd be strange, too. When you know her, you realize she has a heart of gold."

Yes, gold. Hard as rock. "You don't find it a bit more than eccentric the way she's got us chained down here?"

"But that's because she has this strong sense of right and wrong. Papa did teach us good moral values."

I stared into her serene blue eyes. "I'll agree with one thing," I told her, "Papa did quite a job."

I retired to my cot, Veronica could use a little help herself. When I got loose, I'd go to the Human Relations Service and get first-class advice. Maybe McLean Sanitarium would be the place, assuming that they had the money to pay the freight. I'd waive my charges against Florence—what good would a jail term do the poor soul? But she couldn't be left here, who could tell who she might find next to fill her penance stalls?

I hadn't smoked for years but suddenly, in the worst way, I longed for a cigarette. I kept eying the right corner by the door, my leverage spot, I'd go for the arms . . . come on, Knute, you're being quixotic just because she's a little old lady, you've got to clip her one on the chin because only then can you be sure . . . but what if I knocked her out and she fell away from the door? I wouldn't be able to reach her to get the keys, she'd just lie there and come to and be twice as careful . . . hell, I had to wait until she opened the door to my cell. I *had* to get her to open that door.

Maybe she'd open it to bring the dinner in.

She hadn't unlocked it at breakfast time, merely passed it through.

Suppose I played sick, lay on my bunk and groaned?

She'd say get up, here's your supper.

I'd say, I can't, I've got terrible pains.

She'd say, where? Her voice would be anxious.

I'd say, in my head. Get her good and worried as to the damage she'd done with that flashlight. I'd moan more loudly and thrash around.

Oh dear, she'd say, fumbling for her keys. As she did, she'd ask Veronica if I'd been complaining long and Veronica would say . . .

I began to moan, softly at first, building up.

"What's the matter?" asked Veronica.

"I've got pains in my head," I told her. "Oh. O-oh-oh!"

"Oh, dear." Veronica took the bait. "Do lie still. Maybe the pain will go away."

"Maybe." Another groan, pause, not too much too soon.

By the time Florence arrived and the drama had gotten to the point where she asked, "How long has he been carrying on like this?" Veronica answered, "Hours, it seems. Oh, Florence, do you think he might die?"

I moaned and thrashed, waiting for the move to the door, the turn of the key, the entrance, I was ready, yes, indeed, I was ready.

"How should I know?" asked Florence. "I'm no doctor. Well, if he's that sick he won't be able to eat. I'll take his tray back upstairs and eat it myself, it's sirloin strips with fresh mushrooms, our own mushrooms, Veronica!"

"Oh, Goody!"

Oh, God.

❖❖❖❖❖❖❖❖

To say that I awoke hungry on Christmas morning would be understanding the fact. I could have eaten anything—I even went so far as to remove the wooden feed box from the wall just to see if a grain or two of oats or rye or whatever might remain. Knute Severson, thespian par excellence! Knute Severson, starving thespian! Knute Severson, thirsty thespian! Knute Severson, jerk with a capital J!

I knew it was morning because my watch said 6:03 and I could read what my watch said because the light in the corner was on. It had been out, but it must have just come on and that had awakened me. A master switch, of course. Probably at the top of the stairs. Florence was up and doing, damn her hide.

I studied the lay of the land—the light bulb was not bright enough to dispel all the shadows of this winter morning, it was screwed into an old-fashioned electric fixture of white porcelain, and the cloth-covered wires running down the wall had been installed God knows when. We'd found cellar wiring like that at 20 Howe Street when we moved in, but we'd replaced it with Romex in metal coils. Actually, though, I was grateful for the dim inefficiency. If I stationed myself in that corner she might not spot me immediately when she opened the door. No, wait, better to appear to be on the bed, this corner would be better.

There I lay plotting the physical assault of Miss Florence Draggon (height—maybe five feet three or four; age—maybe sixty-five) and I lay feeling like an absolute ass. Although I'd been trained to be polite to little old ladies, in my years with the force I'd seen plenty of little old ladies who'd trip a cripple on crutches. Florence intended to keep me penned, it seemed, until it suited her to let me go. To hell with that!

One vital question. She had to have the key to the leg

shackle with her, had to—or I was nowhere. Obviously, she'd have the key to the stall, she'd need that to get in, but that wasn't a problem anyway. If I weren't caught by the chain I could climb out, jimmy or break the cellar door, assuming it was locked, too, and take my choice of upstairs doors or windows. But I couldn't do a damn thing until I had two free legs.

What were the chances that she'd have the key? I examined the steel cuff and wondered if she kept it oiled and polished, there was not a spot of rust on it, nor on the chain. There was a keyhole in the cuff, a neat small keyhole by keyhole standards. I wondered if I could spring it with my miniature nail-file and scissors set? I had my hand in my pocket, ready to try, when I heard the cellar door open and heard Florence's cheery voice calling, "Merry Christmas! Merry Christmas! Everybody rise and shine!"

I thought of Brenda and Lief and the Christmas tree and the way things should be and I gritted my teeth before I went, obediently, to take the water for washing up from her cautious hands. "Breakfast will be ready in fifteen minutes." She beamed at me and her blue eyes sparkled and her little white curls framed her fat little face and I thought sincerely, Lady, I'm going to belt you the first chance I get.

She returned on schedule, humming "Hark! the Herald Angels Sing." Christmas breakfast consisted of pancakes and sausages all awash in good maple syrup. I hated to admit it, but Miss Draggon could cook better than Brenda and my mother put together. God, it tasted good, and with every bite I felt my strength come back.

I set the empty tray and the night bucket a fair distance back from the door. I wanted her to come all the way in.

"You haven't wished me a merry Christmas, Mr. Severson," Veronica complained.

"I don't feel like wishing anyone a merry Christmas."

She sighed. "I know, but . . . one must observe the amenities no matter what the situation, don't you agree?"

"All right. Merry Christmas. For whatever it's worth. How can you take this kind of treatment, Mrs. Digby? How can you be so passive?"

"What can I do, Mr. Severson? Florence is very strong-minded. She got that from Papa. And she is my only living relative."

Now it was my turn to sigh. "Listen, don't give up. Maybe there is something I can do . . ." I broke off because I heard her coming.

This time Florence was humming "O Little Town of Bethlehem."

I crouched, tense and ready.

She went to Veronica's stall. I heard the jingle of keys—keys, plural! Chances were the keys were on one single ring. Things were looking up—so far, so good, but only so far. . . .

"You should see the yule bird," she told us, "a big tom

turkey, he's browning beautiful. I hope you'll be good and hungry. Veronica, you didn't eat all your breakfast."

"I'm saving my appetite," said Veronica. "You know how I love your oyster and chestnut stuffing."

"Isn't that sweet of you?" Her voice was happy, light. "Did you hear that unsolicited testimonial, Chief Severson?"

"Yes, sounds great."

"I'll be back in a minute for your tray, I can't carry everything at once, you know."

I had a sudden thought, nothing ventured, etc. "Since it's Christmas and you're cooking this fancy meal, how about letting us eat it upstairs?"

"Oh," Veronica chimed in, "that would be a treat, Florence!"

"I don't believe Papa would approve, Veronica. Do you remember the time I had to stay down even though it was my birthday? What had I done that I was being punished for, Sister? Do you recall?"

"Was that the time you bought the Tangee lipstick and Papa found out you'd been wearing it to school?"

"Perhaps. It was so long ago, I've forgotten. Now, don't go away, Chief Severson"—Florence laughed merrily—"I'll be right back."

Hurry up, I thought, hurry up, hurry up.

She seemed to take forever, but finally she unlocked my door (the current carol was "Away in a Manger") and peered in.

"Push your tray a little forward, please," she said, breaking off the humming.

"I can't, my chain's wrapped around the cot leg and I can't get it loose. Can you give me a hand with it?"

She looked for me, found me in my corner looking innocent and trapped. "Oh, I believe you can manage that yourself if you really try." She came in, reached down for the tray, "Papa always said . . ."

Because she was leaning down, my blow caught her flush on the temple and she went down, scattering tray, dishes and bucket.

She went down and lay there. I turned her over, ignoring Veronica, who was crying, "What happened? Florence, are you all right? What happened?"

Florence was wearing an apron over her dress. The apron had pockets. In one pocket was a bunch of keys. I held them toward the light. Yes, there was a little brass one, yes, it looked the right side. "Calm down," I told Veronica. "I'll have you out of here in a minute."

I inserted the key, it fitted, it turned, the anklet fell off. Veronica was still babbling and I kept saying, "I'm coming, I'm coming. Everything's all right."

I unlocked the padlock on her stall and swung the door open. I noted fleetingly that her cubicle was better outfitted than mine—there was, of all things, a Persian carpet on the cement floor. "Okay," I said, "let's have the leg iron," and I knelt on the oriental rug to unlock it.

Then the roof fell in. The last thing I remembered was the red and blue design on the carpet.

❖❖❖❖❖❖❖

So much for Christmas Day.

When I awoke I had the giant monster-sized, huge family-sized headache of headaches. It was more than a headache, it was a big, fat lump of pure pain sitting on my shoulders. Where was I, back on my cot? The world was pitch black. No light, no sound. No point of reference except—quilt? Yes. Cot? Yes. What else? Headache, oh yes. But something else. Ankle. Right ankle. Metal cuff. Shackled again. No, not the same, not the same at all. Caught up tight. Could only move ankle, what—six inches? Eight inches? Seven inches? Couldn't tell. Went back to dark world.

Next outing. Light on. Voices. Female voices. Easy rhythm. How about ankle? Eight inches? No, ten. Definitely. Very tired. Sleep.

Third time around.

Head working better.

Take it easy.

What the hell happened?

Someone speaking. To me. "Chief Severson?" And then, to someone else. "He may die, Veronica. If so, well, how much time will you owe?"

"Miss Draggon." My voice did not, I repeat, did not, sound like mine. "I'm hungry."

"Did you hear that, Veronica? He's hungry. Perhaps he won't die after all. How about some chicken soup, young man? Actually, it's turkey soup but that's just as good. Made from the carcass of the yule bird. I've got a big pot of it. You just wait right there and I'll bring it down."

"Do you dare go into him, Florence? He may attack you again."

"In his condition? What can he do?"

She was so right. On both counts. The turkey soup was just as good as chicken, maybe better. And I couldn't do a damn thing. She even had to feed me.

Time passed. If it weren't for the fact that my watch was a self-winding one with the day's date, I wouldn't have known that the first moment I began to feel better was at 3:30 P.M. (had to be P.M. because the light was on) on December 29.

I cared enough about my personal world to check my head (bandaged, quite neatly) and my shackled leg. No question, the chain was shorter, I had only enough to put both feet on the floor at the side of the cot and stand up. Standing up was a short-lived action, I sat quite quickly. Legs weak; head light but fairly painless.

"Mr. Severson!" Veronica sounded elated. "You're up. How are you feeling?"

"Better. No thanks to you. What did you hit me with?"

"The feed box. I'm sorry, I didn't realize it was so heavy. It was the only thing handy."

"What's the idea of the short chain?"

"Florence didn't think you should roam about so she shortened it. Papa installed the chains with a device that could adjust the length. George said it was a winch like they have on boats. Papa was quite inventive."

"I guess so. Mrs. Digby, why did you hit me when I was trying to help? Do you *like* being penned up down here?"

"In a way, I guess I do. I mean, it's right, do you understand? Are you a Catholic? We're not but they do have some good ideas. If you do something wrong, you pay a penance and then you feel better."

"What the devil did you do that requires this kind of penance?"

"Well, for one thing, I left Papa and Mama and Florence . . ."

"You told me that was years ago!"

"That only makes it worse, don't you see? There was another reason I couldn't let you get away."

"Oh?"

"Don't think I don't know the trouble Florence would get into. I fully realize that a lot of people don't see things as clearly as we do. I couldn't allow Florence to be put in jail, so I just couldn't let you get away. And then, you did strike her. Gentlemen don't strike ladies."

I wasn't going to waste words or energy on that one. I knew the score now. Both of them were as soft as overripe grapes. Regular rules do not apply. Checkmate—and what was my next move? Take your time on this one, Knute, your head may not be up to a third mistake.

So I lay back, like a rape victim, and tried to enjoy it. Much easier advised than done. I spent a lot of time mentally blasting the Wellesley police force. I'd been missing six days and they'd been, I could see it, running around like hound dogs who'd lost their sense of smell.

Then I zeroed in on Mrs. Roberts. Why hadn't she telephoned the station, as she did almost weekly, with another complaint? During which she could blast me out for not getting back to her after the last call. What last call? Why, Christmas Eve when I told him about the pornographic snowman. What snowman? The snowman at that Draggon woman's house. . . . Why didn't Mrs. Roberts ring her bell and alert the countryside?

All right, leave that. Brenda. Brenda was going through hell. I don't know which bothered me the most, my personal situation or Brenda's distress. Lief wouldn't understand—oh, he'd know something was wrong, but I knew Brenda would handle that in the right way. And that thought led me to this thought: what if I'd been killed in an accident or line of duty? How had I left things? Not so shipshape, now that I had time to reflect. When I got out of this mess, I'd talk to Gary Lyons about that. When I got out of this mess. If I got out of this mess?

I faced it. Were the ladies crazy enough to kill me? I was no medico but I'd bet they'd come close to it already. An inch or two in one direction or another with that feed box and it could have been bye-bye Knute. Also, let's not forget that Florence had my gun. To tell the truth, at the beginning I'd been inclined to look upon this adventure as a monstrous joke on me. But I was no longer laughing.

Florence brought meals and treated me with courtesy. I treated her likewise. Awakening the morning of the thirtieth, I felt much better. In fact, I felt well enough to take a clear-eyed look at my options. Options? Pro-Knute: I was alive, I was feeling pretty good—physically, that is. Anti-Knute: Florence and Veronica had many reasons, some sane, some not so sane, to keep me—forever? I was chained and boxed and contained and I had no weapons—I'd noticed that my feed box had disappeared—no turn and turnabout.

The only thing I did have was that little nail file-scissor gadget that Brenda had given me. Not exactly the best tool for digging mortar out of rocks or filing chain links.

On the trays Florence brought were forks and spoons—if there was meat, it came precut. Florence would have made a good prison guard. She'd pulled another fast deal—the chain was kept taut until she'd placed the food tray inside the stall, then eased so that I could reach the tray. Vice versa for retrieving tray and/or bucket. Papa had been, indeed, an inventive man. Status remained quo. But that didn't mean a mistake wouldn't be made, sooner or later, and I meant to be ready for that mistake.

I set about getting my facts straight. Veronica had been in her place of penance for over six months, if I could believe what she said; she hadn't been upstairs or outside at all. Therefore, it had been Florence playing either the role of Florence or, with wig and accessories, of Veronica, who had triggered Mrs. Roberts' wrath and who had talked with me. Why? Mental aberration, of course; I could imagine that Florence had a heavy resentment of Veronica, the one who got away. Not only got away, but stayed away and got married and lived the life that, presumably, ladies of their age and station expected to live. So, what the hell, she acted out the Veronica role, making sure that the Veronica person got the blame for any Florence capers. And making up Veronica stories about travel and excitement, stories that Florence would like to, but never would, act out.

As for Veronica, she'd explained her position logically— logically, that is, if you'd had a Papa like Papa. Jesus, what a job that old boy had done on his daughters.

But—was that all? Was a weird setup like this that simple? No way. Why was Florence so kind and considerate of her prisoner? Because she was naturally kind and considerate? She had all the milk of human kindness of a nurse shark. So, why?

Fattening up for something? Correct choice of verb—

her meals and no exercise were beginning to show up, my belt was loosened one notch. My belt? Leather, brass buckle. Could I do anything with my belt? Use it like a whip? Snap, from the bed, and the buckle makes contact with skull. . . . I could practice, maybe, without Veronica catching on, or take a chance with a first try . . . hold it, Knute. What good would that do? The mechanism that tightened the chain was outside the wall and the chain would prevent me from getting to her unless I could lure her, close, close . . . aha, put that one in the safe, Knute, for future use.

I swear Florence had ESP or maybe there was a new look in my eye when she brought lunch because she gave me that jolly smile and announced, "By the way, I don't carry the keys to the ankle chain around with me anymore. It's for your sake, actually, Chief Severson. Papa always said keep temptation away from those who can't handle it."

Begging wasn't my field, but I wasn't too old to learn. "Miss Draggon, you'd be doing us all a favor if you let me out of here. I know you're concerned about what will happen to you, but I assure you that I'll be on your side. We'll get a good doctor and work this thing out. . . . I assure you, I have no personal animosity . . ."

She dimpled at me. "You are a sweet boy. I know you mean well, but I don't think even your good offices could save Veronica from death row, or whatever they call it."

"I told you, Florence," Veronica interrupted, "the death penalty has been abolished. It's life imprisonment now."

Florence made a fierce gesture. "All right! Life imprisonment. Would you like that? Being locked up for the rest of your life? How would you like that?"

There was something blackly comic about this conversation but I let that go. "It sounds as though you're talking about homicide," I said carefully. "It sounds to me as though Veronica killed somebody."

"But not on purpose!" Veronica was indignant. "I loved George, I didn't mean to really hurt him. It was just that he was so critical of Florence, he was like you, he kept insisting that she needed a doctor and he was going to call one—he actually had his hand on the telephone, and I said sharply, George, don't do that, please don't do that, we can manage everything in the family as we always have but he just shook his head and began to dial so I had to stop him, didn't I? Didn't I, Florence? I picked up Papa's curly maple walking stick, I didn't know it had lead in the knob—how would I know that, he got it after I left home?" She stared at us wide-eyed.

"So you hit your husband with the walking stick." I spelled it out. "On the head, I presume, since both of you specialize in blunt weapons and craniums. Whereupon George fell down dead. Tell me"—I was really curious—"how did you fox a doctor? It's pretty hard to cover up a fractured skull."

"Oh"—Florence waved plump hands airily—"we didn't

call a doctor. We're not very fond of doctors. Papa said most of them were charlatans."

"Then—how did you bury him? You can't dispose of a body without a death certificate."

"Silly boy." Florence smoothed her apron smugly. "We buried him in Papa's place."

"In Papa's place? You mean, in your father's grave?"

"I mean in the grave that was to have been Papa's grave. Down here. Out there." And she pointed beyond my cell.

"You mean Veronica's husband is buried in this cellar?"

"Well not now . . ." Veronica began but Florence cut her off.

"It was the perfect spot. Papa didn't want to be placed in a public cemetery, you see. Papa wanted to remain in his house with his family so he left an uncemented space at the end of the cellar for his grave. We were going to put a rail around it, make a little private shrine, you must know how pretty they can be. But"—her tone became injured—"they wouldn't let Mama and me bury Papa where he, where we, wished. But"—she brightened—"it turned out for the best after all because then we had a place for George."

"Hold it a minute. What did you mean, Veronica, that he isn't there now?"

Veronica looked pleadingly at her sister. "I mean, he's gone . . . I mean, when one dies he's gone. You know what I mean."

"What she means is"—Florence went purposefully to the door—"is that we had to get rid of George to make room for the other man. Have a good lunch, Chief Severson. What do the Europeans say? *Bon appétit.*"

◆◆◆◆◆◆◆◆

"Wait," I called to Florence, now closing the door behind herself, "what other man?" I thought I knew but I had to hear the name.

She was smiling, as usual, but her blue eyes were cold. "That fat fool who came poking around a few weeks back. Said he was a town official, said that Roberts woman on Schaller Street had called him and complained about us. Grinned at me like a slice of watermelon and he was sure we could straighten out this little misunderstanding. Said maybe the solution was to sell our house and land and move. Said we'd get a lot of money for our place and that he knew of a perfect place for us, he'd handle the whole thing. Said it as though we had no choice. That's the other man."

"Hugo Hix."

"Yes. That was his name."

"He's dead then."

"He's buried." She shrugged.

"How did it happen?"

A glint of amusement chased the ice from her eyes. "I offered to show him the house. I started with the cellar."

"The flashlight bit?"

"No, no. That wasn't heavy enough. I used a log. There's a pile cut for fireplaces at the bottom of the steps, you didn't notice. The one I chose was of elm, from a diseased tree we cut down a couple of years back. It burned very nicely."

"I see. Then you didn't mean to put me out of the way permanently or you would have used a log?"

"No. I didn't." Was I wrong, or was there unusual emphasis on *didn't?*

Still, I couldn't let it alone. "Why? Surely I'm more of a problem alive."

"That's true. I just didn't feel—the hatred. You had better manners." She looked suddenly, grotesquely arch. "And you were so good-looking."

Past tenses. I *didn't* feel the hatred. You *had* better manners. You *were* good-looking.

"And now?" I asked softly. I now shared several secrets.

"Enjoy your lunch," she said and left.

I ate slowly, thinking. "How did she get rid of Hugo's car?" I asked Veronica.

"Who? Oh, the other man's? She said she drove it to a place where many cars were parked and left it there."

"How'd she get back?"

Veronica giggled. "She hitchhiked. She'd never done that before. She said a young man with a beard picked her up who told her she was really heavy. Florence was offended, she's not thin, you know, but then the young man explained that heavy had nothing to do with weight, was a compliment. So, by the time he'd left her in Natick Square, she decided she liked hitchhiking. She thinks maybe she'd like to try it again." Veronica picked up a piece of ham on her fork. "But she won't."

"Why?"

"Papa wouldn't have approved."

I swallowed a few more bites. "What did you do with George? Had he ever, by the way, been in the Navy?"

"Oh yes, George was in the Navy when I met him. It was wartime, you know. He looked so handsome in his dress blues." She blinked a couple of times, her voice blurred. "Florence didn't tell me what she did with George. I was very upset about moving George to make space for the other man, but Florence pointed out that George had been dead long enough so that she doubted anyone could tell how it happened, while the new one wouldn't fool a soul. He could even, she said, be traced to the house, and that, she said, would never do because then they'd find out about George, too, and we'd both be in trouble." She looked up at me with pale blue eyes, suddenly sad, suddenly aware. "We are in trouble, aren't we?"

I nodded. I felt sorry for her but not sorry enough. Florence had, I guessed, dragged George's body to the river during the brief thaw. The Charles backed up to Schaller Lane. She was a shrewdie, she probably figured the river would freeze again quickly and he wouldn't be found until spring. But she'd miscalculated; George had surfaced. Just the same, Florence's batting average was pretty good. Two dead men and nobody knew but me.

That was the bad news.

Where was the good news?

At six thirty-five Veronica said, "Florence is late."

"Hmm?" I'd been thinking hard about something else.

"It's after six-thirty, isn't it? Or is my watch fast? I was just saying that Florence is late with dinner."

I checked my watch: six thirty-six. "Only a few minutes late." I'd had the glimmering of an idea but it was pretty iffy. If this worked, if that happened then . . .

"It isn't like her. To be late for dinner."

"Maybe she's cooking something special."

"She'd plan it so that it would be ready."

I looked upward at the cobwebs and pipes. "Maybe somebody came to call." If I had a long pole I could bang it against the ceiling, which had to be the floor of—I didn't have any idea what part of the house we were situated under. And I didn't have a long pole.

"That must be it." Veronica relaxed.

I kept staring upward. Not a sound. A well-built house, damn it. Suppose I yelled. It wouldn't hurt to try. I began to shout. "Hey! Hey! Up there, hey!"

"What on earth are you doing?" Veronica wanted to know.

I ignored her. "Help! Help! Down cellar! Help!"

"You're hurting my ears," Veronica protested.

"Shut up." I was listening, listening hard. Nothing. I began, louder, as loud as I could yell. I kept it up. If I had something to throw at the ceiling, a rock, a hunk of wood, something. But I hadn't. And I was getting hoarse but that was all I was getting. After a while I shut up and just sat there.

"I could have told you that wouldn't do any good." Veronica's tone held mild censure. "Once when I was a girl I screamed at Papa for ages and Florence said they never heard a sound. And another time Florence cried for two days, at least she told me she did, and I didn't hear her either even though I was right upstairs a lot of the time."

"Okay, okay. I got the message."

"Whoever it is, I wish they'd hurry and go. I'm getting hungry."

I grunted in reply, rubbed at my shackled ankle. The metal had worn a hole right through my sock and was chafing the skin. The least of my problems.

"What time is it? My watch says seven o'clock. Is that possible?"

I grunted again.

"Oh, dear." She sighed and was silent. She spoke again in fifteen minutes, fifteen minutes on the dot, the same question: where was Florence?

By seven-thirty she'd decided that something was

definitely wrong. "She could be ill. She could have fallen. She may be lying up there helpless . . ."

I laughed bitterly, I'll admit. "So what could we do if she were?"

Veronica sniffed tearfully. "You aren't any comfort at all. The least you could do is tell me that she isn't sick, that she hasn't hurt herself."

"Oh, I can do that all right."

"Then what is keeping her? What is she doing?"

"She's thinking. She's figuring things out."

"Figuring what out?"

"She's realized that she's put herself in jeopardy. She's wishing that she'd never invited this particular fly into her parlor. She sees that, while each of you killed a man, you are guilty of manslaughter while she committed murder. She finally understands that she's in real danger."

Veronica's face crumpled. "Danger? From whom?"

"From me. From you."

"From me?"

"Of course. Who knows about George and Hugo? You and I."

"But Florence is my dear sister, I would never tell anybody . . ."

"You told me."

"So did she!"

"True. Too true. She wishes she hadn't. But it's done and now she's figuring out how to eliminate the danger."

Unshed tears shone in Veronica's eyes and her mouth was an O. She gulped. "How will she do that?"

"I'm not sure. I think she's already begun in the simplest way there is."

"The . . . simplest . . . way?"

"She's just going to forget we're down here."

"She wouldn't. She wouldn't!" The tears were no longer unshed.

"Time will tell," I said coldly.

But the litany continued, Florence wouldn't, she wouldn't leave us without food or water, Florence was hurt, Florence was sick, that's what had happened, Florence was lying up there helpless and couldn't come to us. . . .

At 9 P.M. the lights went out. Veronica stopped in mid-sentence and we sat silently for a moment in the darkness.

"At least," I said softly, "she's able to get to the light switch."

❖❖❖❖❖❖❖

Well, we kept hoping she'd reconsider. Veronica spent a lot of time crying. I sent my mind scurrying, a rat in a maze; there must be a way out.

How long could a human being live without food? More important, how long without liquid? I'd never gone into the subject, but I'd read somewhere that thirst was the real specter. Had I read—five days? Ten? I couldn't recall, or maybe I didn't want to recall?

The lights came on in the morning, but no Florence. Physically I felt hungry, good and hungry but not starving, not yet. It was early morning and I'd missed one meal the day before, I'd gone without one meal a time or two. I wondered how long it would be until I was as ravenous as the day after I'd attacked Florence. I blamed that irrational hunger on my injury, because all my energies had been busy directing antibodies, I'd needed fuel but quick. But now that I was well fed and well rested, I figured it would take longer to starve to death. My good thought for the day—or was it? Because, God, I was thirsty. And I don't mean by that I just wanted a drink of water. I *needed* a drink of water—bad.

"Veronica? Are you awake? How are you feeling?"

"She'll come with breakfast, you'll see. And she'll have something special to make up for it, that's the way she is."

Poor, trusting Veronica. How had she ever had the guts to get away? Maybe she'd been different when younger, with more spirit. I started to say don't bet on it, decided not to dash her hopes, changed my mind again when she began talking about juice and strong coffee and eggs in butter.

"Veronica, stop it. She isn't coming. We have to find a way out of here. You have to help. Is there anything you haven't told me?"

"Told you? What do you mean?"

"I don't know what I mean in this crazy place, it could

be anything, a door that moves when you say 'open sesame,' how do I know?"

"Why, Mr. Severson, of course there isn't any such thing. Papa was not a frivolous man. When he had this house built, he built it to last. The best materials, the best workmen, Papa believed in the best. It was rather new in those days but Papa put in plumbing and electricity, he was a man of vision. He said this house will last my children and my grandchildren. Of course, he doesn't have any grandchildren, but the house will endure. Doors that move to open sesame, indeed. If he'd ever heard you say such a thing he'd have thought you were crazy.

The glimmering of an idea I'd had the night before sparked anew. Under the circumstances, it was possible.

I had a tool—of sorts. The file-scissor's length was maybe two—two and a half inches. Such as it was, it was asset one. Asset two, the quilt. Both to be used only in case of desperation and desperation was slowly but surely raising its ugly head.

But—what if it didn't work?

I'd have shot my wad but it was, so far as I could see, the only wad I had.

Wait? Wait a little longer? Wait for some kind fate to intervene, for Florence to have a change of heart?

I waited. I didn't like the waiting. I wanted to get the hell out of there.

Still, I waited. Until the middle of the afternoon when Veronica couldn't seem to stop crying. By then I'd remembered that tomorrow was the first day of the New

Year, a holiday, and it would be next to impossible to get an electrician. Maybe I'd waited too long already.

The old-time, cloth-wrapped—what kind of cloth had they used, asbestos?—wires from the light high in the corner of the stall ran down the side of the wall in the corner near the end of my cot. I managed to get the quilt wrapped around my chest and arms, just testing, yes, I could use my hands enough. But I was pretty clumsy holding the file through the quilt so I dropped it and started out bare-handed.

Careful, now. Run the file over the asbestos, whatever, scrape it away from a wire. Come on, separate, damn you, don't get overanxious, Knute, don't break the delicate little file. There, one wire gleamed. I shredded the covering, bent it upward and away.

Then I went to work on the second one. I was perspiring and my hands were sweaty. Across the way Veronica moaned.

There. At last, how long had it taken, five minutes? It seemed like an hour. Two bare wires awaited my pleasure. I took up the quilt, pulled it up to my chin, puffed it out there so that I could duck behind it. If my plan worked, there would be sparks, how dangerous they would be I didn't know but I was taking no chances.

Peering over the edge, hands covered by the quilt, I moved the two wires together.

A blue flame shot up the wire, sizzled, and my light went out. When I emerged from behind the quilt everything was dark and Veronica's light was out too.

"What . . . ?" she wailed, an unintelligible sound,

then, "What happened? What happened? Mr. Severson, are you there? What happened?"

"I hope," I replied grimly, "that I shorted the whole damned electrical system."

"But, why? Why did you do that? I don't like the dark. I'm afraid!"

Had it worked? Down here it had, but what about upstairs? She wouldn't get an electrician on the double unless she lost lights and heat. The oil burner worked off an electric thermostat. No power, no heat. How long would it be before I knew?

We sat there. I told Veronica my theory, my hope, and she had nothing to say to that other than, "I don't understand." After that, we silently waited.

Assume the worst. I'd blown a fuse, the one to the cellar, which had been a separate fuse and nothing else of importance had been put out of action. If so, we'd sit and wait literally until doomsday.

Look on the bright side. It was an old electrical system, maybe the original, which Papa had "built to last." Therefore the single-line system had blown and she was waiting, as we were, for the arrival of the electrician. When the electrician came, he would have to come into the cellar to find the cause of the shortage. That was my hope. My sincere hope.

My gamble was two-edged. A, the system hadn't blow and I wouldn't have a second chance; B, she'd take care of us before the electrician came. How? Well, she had my gun. I wouldn't put anything past her. I knew her now.

But what else could I do?

I heard my silent question and thought, My God, I sound like an old woman. They've made me one of them.

We sat there. I don't know how long; I couldn't see the face of my watch. Fifteen minutes? Thirty? An hour?

Veronica said, "I smell smoke."

I sniffed. The unmistakable acrid odor confirmed Veronica's statement.

"Jesus Christ," I said reverently, "I've set the house on fire."

"That must be because of the penny."

"Because of—the what?"

"The penny. Papa taught us to put a penny behind any fuse that blew. Florence does that, every time. George told Florence that was dangerous because the reason the fuse blew was to tell you there was something wrong and the penny stopped that from happening . . ." Her voice sharpened. "The house is on fire? Oh, dear Father! We'll be roasted to death!"

"We'll die of asphyxiation first," I said grimly. Fire. I felt like laughing wildly, I'd remembered a song: "Christmas is coming, the goose is getting fat, please put a penny in the old man's hat. If you haven't got a penny, then a ha'penny will do. If you haven't got a ha'penny, then God bless you!" That was funny, that was, wasn't that funny? Christmas come and Christmas gone and we were left with the penny . . . "When a ha'penny would do," I found myself humming, caught myself.

"I wish"—Veronica gave a half sigh, half sob—"I weren't so hungry. I wouldn't mind so much on a full stomach . . ."

"Mrs. Digby, shut up. You're wasting oxygen."

"I don't understand, I don't understand how it's come to this. Just because I wanted a life of my own, if I hadn't run away and then brought George back, there'd be none of this! I'm willing to accept my punishment but I don't want to burn to death . . . oh, Papa, please . . . I don't want to . . . I'm so afraid, Papa . . ." The hysterical words blurred into unintelligible snufflings, whispered prayers. Poor ruined creature, I thought with a strange detachment that clued me. I was getting light-headed. I was standing off somewhere, watching the scene with studied interest.

"The danger"—my voice sounded far away to my ears—"is from the smoke. Be quiet. Let me think. The quilts—if we make tents of the quilts, will that help? Keep the air cleaner, the little air trapped inside the quilt . . . ?" The smell of smoke was stronger, I could see it gray against the darkness.

"Florence!" Veronica screeched the word. "Florence! Where are you? Come let us out!"

Yes, where was she? Was she upstairs fighting flames, calling the fire department? Had she fled the house and the fire? Where was the fire anyway? Was it a big fire? Was it smoldering inside the partitions, to be smelled but not seen? I couldn't hear a damn thing but Veronica . . . would her crazy sister run, leaving us to . . . Yes, she would. Of course she would. How could she let anyone find us? No one in their right mind would . . . would what? Besides, she wasn't in her right mind. Was I? Make a tent of the quilt. . . . I coughed, got a noseful, the whole house might be filled with smoke, maybe she'd been lying down, napping, and the smoke had gotten to her, in which case there was no hope, no hope at all.

How had I gotten into this mess?

I told Veronica to make a tent and I hid under my quilt. It was pitch black in there, and in this confining little cloth world of patchwork pieces my lungs hurt, I coughed; my eyes smarted, smarted . . . smart I was not because if I were I'd never taken the chance . . . man bouncing around like a crazy atom, bumped into crazier atom, fireworks, fire . . . works . . .

Somebody screaming, Veronica screaming, yelling. No use, shut up. Help, help, help. I'm moving on to some other place where there are voices, male voices, a man's world out there, up there . . .

Something pulled my tent away, someone shone a bright light upon me.

"Mother of God!" said a loud, startled voice. "It's Severson!"

❖❖❖❖❖❖❖

Darkness: is darkness the lack of all color? And white the presence of all color? I opened my eyes and coughed. My chest hurt, the brightness danced wildly.

"Dearling." Brenda's voice. Hand on mine, Brenda's hand. Body lying prone on bed. Ceiling, walls white, square of black night—window. Hospital. Thank God. Hospital.

"Glad New Year," I said, and went away.

When I came back, Brenda was still there, I was still in a hospital bed in a hospital room, there was an oxygen tank beside my bed, not now in use, and Dennehy stood near the oxygen tank looking just as solid, just as potentially useful.

"How am I?" I asked.

"Better." Brenda looked pale, tired.

"Veronica?"

"Down the hall," Dennehy answered. His voice sounded funny, wobbly. "She'll be okay."

"Florence called the fire department." I found that fact surprising.

Brenda said, "Thank God," but Dennehy knew why. "You'd have thought that house was a person. Papa's house, Papa's house, that's all she'll say. She was running around outside with a garden hose when they got there."

"Hugo. Hugo is down there. Buried."

Brenda's hand tightened on mine.

"They found Hugo. They'd marked the hole in the cellar with a blank tombstone, would you believe it?" Dennehy's tone was wondering.

"Papa's stone."

"Old man Draggon? Dunno, no marking on it. When

the fire department got the fire out, after they got you out, the fire marshal came investigating. Maybe you don't know, the fire started in the paneling, old wiring, the whole place was a firetrap. O'Reilly said they were lucky to contain the blaze in the upper floors, as it is it's half gutted.

"I set the fire."

I saw Dennehy shoot a quick glance at Brenda, I could hear her gasp. I saw, too, that he hadn't planned on telling her all the details. I always told Brenda most things. . . . Why would Dennehy be holding back? Unless he thought I'd acted strangely. . . . I wanted to ask him what he would have done, but of course I couldn't, of course I never would.

They kept me in the hospital for nearly a week, my ankle was rubbed raw from the chain, I was dehydrated, a little concussed and slightly smoke-damaged. I got out as soon as I could; I'd had enough visitors, for one thing.

Most of the men from the department came, almost all of them informed me that my car and gun had been recovered. Told me with eyes averted. The selectmen came with Sowerby, they brought red roses and considered compliments calculated to make me proud.

Chip Dawher brought his wife and a pen and paper. "The whole story, Knute, old man. Boy were they ever right when they said truth was stranger than fiction! The Boston papers have gone gaga and the Associated Press is nagging me for your statement. I'm telling you, you're front-page stuff."

I'd been feeling better until then. I told him tersely that Florence Draggon would be charged with the murder of Hugo Hix; that Veronica Digby would be given a lesser charge in the death of her husband, "but I don't know if we'll get to court. The district attorney has his doubts, pleas of insanity . . . that's not for publication, of course."

"I know all that." The Dawhers sat side by side, studying me with vicarious interest. "It's your story they want. 'Police Chief Prisoner of Two Little Old Ladies' . . . that kind of thing." Dawher grinned. "You'll probably end up on Sonja Hamlin's program. Or even Johnny Carson."

I felt like socking somebody, but he was the only one handy so I didn't. I said, "No way," and seethed inside.

Miss Miller came, bringing a poinsettia. "I never would have expected it of her. In school, she was the perfect example, always doing exactly what she was told."

I answered carefully, "That was her problem."

Now her eyes found me, skidded off.

"You don't mean that, surely. It's right to obey rules. That's the trouble with the world today, everybody's always changing the rules. Or paying no mind."

I shook my head wearily. I'd probably never be able to explain to her. "Yes, follow the rules because they make sense. Not simply because you're told to."

She shook her head, doubtfully. "I don't entirely agree.

I remember when I was small, my mother convinced me to do as she said without question. There was, she told me, always a good reason."

I didn't answer that a good rule for little children wasn't necessarily a good rule for adults. I didn't say anything about the seeding of guilt. Miss Miller had, I suspected, lived a life with and for her mama just as Florence had for Papa. But Miss Miller had somehow managed to stay sane, repressed, no doubt, but sane, while Florence and Veronica . . . No doubt the difference lay in Papa. I could still see his stern, stubborn, pictured face, small evil eyes, a mean mouth . . . or had he merely looked like an ordinary man and I imagined the rest? For a while I had nightmares about Papa.

❖❖❖❖❖❖❖

We had Christmas when I got home, which delighted Lief because he'd opened his presents Christmas Day ("I couldn't let him know how terrified I was," Brenda explained, "so I tried to pretend everything was normal."). A second Christmas, of course, called for extra presents for Lief—so what if we were spoiling him?

I was pleased with my gifts, but my biggest present was being home.

My ordeal was out there. Hugo'd had a great big funeral and everybody wanted to talk about it and wanted to know all the details. I can't count how many times I gave the set speech I finally made up.

There were letters to the editor in the *Townsman*. Most of them were laudatory, a few ran along the lines of this one:

"I don't doubt that Chief of Police Knute Severson acted to the best of his ability in the dangerous situation on Schaller Lane, but I do find myself with unanswered questions.

"How well protected are we if the head of our department of public safety cannot recognize serious mental illness when faced with it?

"How well protected are we if our police chief permits himself to be captured and taken prisoner by an elderly woman?

"How well protected are we if the police department is incapable of discovering the whereabouts of its principal officer?

"Even considering the circumstances, is not setting fire to another's personal property an act of calculated arson?

"Rather than accepting the plaudits of the multitude, I should think that Police Chief Severson should be ashamed of himself and I hope he has learned a valuable lesson."

The letter was signed "Sincerely yours, Mrs. Clinton Roberts," and for once Mrs. Roberts was dead right.

I was ashamed of myself.

◆◆◆◆◆◆◆

Late in January, Algernon was as sick as a dog. It seems he got hold of a sack of garbage and ate it and whatever he ate poisoned him. It was serious, the vet only just managed to pull him through. Because of his size, a Saint Bernard requires a lot of poison.

I found the remains of the sack—it was a brown paper bag and there were crumbs in it. Crumbs of gingerbread.

Florence Draggon had given me a brown paper bag of gingerbread men for Lief. I left it in the car and forgot it. Brenda swept out the car after we got it back and the bag went into the trash barrel.

We never did find out for sure what was in the gingerbread men. The vet thinks it was some kind of rat poison.

"That woman!" Brenda's eyes flashed. "That dreadful woman!"

"She was holiday-minded," I said, feeling facetious. "She went in for tricky treats and Christmas clubs."

"Why, Knute, how can you joke about it?"

"Now I can." And perhaps I learned the lesson Mrs. Roberts wanted me to learn: that bad jokes can help take a nasty taste out of your mouth?

"Well, there's one person I'll be eternally grateful to," Brenda was saying.

"Who's that?"

"Doddy Miller. She'd stop by and call just about every day. She was so worried about you. And she's been so nice to Lief."

"Yeah?" You never know, do you? "What's she done for Lief?"

"Brought him all sorts of presents. He didn't understand what happened to Christmas, you know, and if it hadn't been for Doddy's kindness—well, it kept him a rather happy little boy under very trying circumstances."

"She shouldn't be spending her hard-earned money that way," I said, and Brenda shook her head at me.

"She seemed to get such pleasure out of it. And we'll do something nice for her in return, won't we?"

I grinned. "Sure thing. The first thing I plan to do is have a drink—here's to Doddy Miller! Bless her little old-maid heart."